# "Repeat After Me...

"I will spend the next year discovering who I am and what I want out of life."

Catherine felt a sigh building deep inside as she repeated the vow. Her gaze met his. His eyes were filled with longing and regret as he lowered his head slowly until their lips barely met. His arms slid around her waist, strong and possessive and loving. Then he pulled away, his hands lingering at her waist.

"Shall we make another vow before I put you in a cab and send you off to your hotel?"

"Why not?" she said breathlessly.

"Let's make a promise to meet right here next year and see how our lives have changed."

"I'd like that very much."

"Then I'll be waiting for you," he promised.

"Until next year," she whispered. It seemed as close as tomorrow. And as far away as forever.

Dear Reader:

Welcome to the world of Silhouette Desire. Join me as we travel to a land of incredible passion and tantalizing romance—a place where dreams can, and do, come true.

When I read a Silhouette Desire, I sometimes feel as if I'm going on a little vacation. I can relax, put my feet up, and become transported to a new world . . . a world that has, naturally, a perfect hero just waiting to whisk me away! These are stories to remember, containing moments to treasure.

Silhouette Desire novels are romantic love stories—sensuous yet emotional. As a reader, you not only see the hero and heroine fall in love, you also feel what they're feeling.

In upcoming months look for books by some of your favorite Silhouette Desire authors: Joan Hohl, Ann Major, Elizabeth Lowell and Linda Lael Miller.

So enjoy!

Lucia Macro
Senior Editor

# SHERRYL WOODS

## NEXT TIME...FOREVER

SILHOUETTE *Desire*®

Published by Silhouette Books New York

**America's Publisher of Contemporary Romance**

SILHOUETTE BOOKS
300 East 42nd St., New York, N.Y. 10017

ISBN: 0-373-05601-X

First Silhouette Books printing November 1990

**Books by Sherryl Woods**

Silhouette Desire

*Not at Eight, Darling* #309
*Yesterday's Love* #329
*Come Fly with Me* #345
*A Gift of Love* #375
*Can't Say No* #431
*Heartland* #472
*One Touch of Moondust* #521
*Next Time... Forever* #601

Silhouette Special Edition

*Safe Harbor* #425
*Never Let Go* #446
*Edge of Forever* #484
*In Too Deep* #522
*Miss Liz's Passion* #573
*Tea and Destiny* #595

Silhouette Books

*Silhouette Summer Sizzlers* 1990
"A Bridge to Dreams"

---

## SHERRYL WOODS

lives by the ocean, which, she says, provides daily inspiration for the romance in her soul. She further explains that her years as a television critic taught her about steamy plots and humor; her years as a travel editor took her to exotic locations; and her years as a crummy weekend tennis player taught her to stick with what she enjoyed most—writing. "What better way is there," Sherryl asks, "to combine all that experience than by creating romantic stories?"

# Prologue

---

*May 16*

Bold streaks of pink and gold banded the twilight sky and shimmered across the calm surface of the Savannah River. It was a dazzling, postcard-splashy sunset, but the lazy, mournful wail of a ship's horn more accurately reflected Catherine Devlin's mood as she watched the huge freighter inch through the narrow channel.

Sipping a glass of overly-sweet white zinfandel wine, she tried to remember the precise moment when her once storybook-perfect life had gone so terribly wrong. What had been the turning point? When had Matthew fallen out of love with her and turned to other women? Even more disturbing, how had she ever allowed her own dreams to become so overshadowed by her need to please her husband? Everyone thought Mrs. Matthew Devlin was so strong, so clever, but no one really knew *Catherine* Devlin. She didn't even recognize herself anymore.

"More coffee?"

Lost in her private desolation, she waved the waiter away without glancing up. "No, thanks."

"Are you sure?" he said. There was an oddly plaintive note in his deep, rumbly voice that brought her head up. Dark brown eyes that glinted with the devil's own laughter watched her closely.

"It's fresh," he promised, passing the pot temptingly beneath her nose so she could savor the rich aroma.

She found herself breathing deeply, then smiling apologetically into those irresistible, teasing eyes. She pointed to the clean, empty cup beside her plate. "Sorry. I'm not drinking coffee, just wine."

"Oh." He sounded incredibly disappointed and looked as though he couldn't quite make up his mind what to do next.

Catherine found his apparent uncertainty endearing, but oddly out of character. "Are you new?" she asked kindly. Though she'd asked merely to put him at ease, she realized as she was waiting for his reply that she was clinging to the interruption. She was tired of being alone with nothing but her gloomy thoughts for company. Those eyes, so filled with life and humor, were the perfect antidote to her unexpected loneliness.

"You could say that," he agreed, instantly looking more hopeful and twice as appealing. "You're the first person I've waited on."

"Ever?" she said skeptically. Another close examination aroused more puzzling contradictions. He appeared to be in his mid-thirties, too old to be waiting tables for the first time unless he was down on his luck. Yet she found herself dismissing that possibility immediately. There was an undefinable look of success, an aura of confident masculinity about him that seemed just as out of place as his vulnerable demeanor. It was as though she was watching a badly miscast actor struggling to play against type. The incongruities intrigued her.

"My first customer ever," he confirmed. "Are you absolutely sure you wouldn't like some coffee?"

She decided to play the game—if that's what it was—and find out where it led. "Are you trying to see if you can pour without spilling?"

A roguish dimple formed in one cheek. "Actually, I'm trying to find a way to keep talking to you."

The direct, boldly flirtatious response was the last thing she'd expected. Waiters in Atlanta's elite establishments did not make passes at the customers. But then again, she'd rarely dined there alone. Maybe women by themselves were considered fair game.

"Why?" she asked cautiously.

"You're a beautiful woman. You're apparently alone. And you looked so sad that I thought someone ought to cheer you up."

Her gaze narrowed slightly. "You figure you'll get a bigger tip for doing that?"

He shook his head. There was just the tiniest suggestion of guilt in his expression. "No tip." He leaned closer. "If you promise not to tell, I'll confess something."

Increasingly bemused by the entire conversation, Catherine was nonetheless fascinated. She found herself promising. Solemnly. Crossing her heart, in fact. She hadn't done that since she was ten. It felt good to feel young again and to be sharing secrets, especially with a man as devilishly handsome as this one.

He grinned in apparent satisfaction. "I knew I could count on you. Actually," he confided, "I'm not even a waiter. I grabbed the coffeepot on my way past the service station." He pointed toward a strategically placed counter filled with pots of coffee, decaf and hot water, plus an assortment of silverware, napkins and extra salt and pepper shakers.

Falling prey to his teasing tone, she said lightly, "Let me guess. You're a busboy and you're hoping for a promotion."

He laughed. "Wrong. I don't even work here."

Catherine glanced at the coffeepot in his hand, then more closely at his attire. The perfect fit of his charcoal slacks hinted of custom tailoring. The fabric was definitely not polyester. His shirt cuffs were monogrammed, the material some sort of expensive silk and cotton blend. She glanced down. His shoes looked exactly like the last pair she'd bought for Matthew. They'd cost in the neighborhood of two hundred dollars. It was definitely a pricey neighborhood for a busboy or a waiter, even taking into account generous tips.

"Okay, then," she said sternly, wishing she could keep her lips from curving into an all-too-easily-forgiving smile. "It's confession time. What's the real story?"

He feigned a sheepish expression. At least she assumed it was feigned. Now that she'd taken a closer look, he didn't appear to be the type to make explanations for himself.

"I was eating over there all by myself," he confessed, "when I saw you." He gestured toward a table where the remnants of a meal had yet to be cleared away. A matching charcoal jacket had been slung across the back of a chair and a tie draped over that. "I watched you come in and knew I had to meet you. You didn't look like the kind of lady who'd like being picked up in a restaurant, so voilà! The coffee."

"Definitely enterprising," she commended him, surprised to discover that she was enjoying the unexpected flirtation. It had been a very long time since anyone had dared to come on to her, unless they'd been drinking so heavily that the prospect of Matthew's possessive wrath no longer fazed them. This man appeared to be stone-cold sober and openly fascinated. In her present mood, it was a difficult combination to resist.

Catherine propped her chin in her hand and met his gaze evenly. "What kind of lady do I appear to be?" She was honestly curious. The divorce papers still folded in her purse said quite plainly that she was no longer a wife. Without that role, she wasn't so sure what she actually was anymore. Maybe this stranger could give her a clue as to what Catherine Devlin had become.

"Classy," he said at once, pleasing her. "Self-contained. Maybe a little lost."

"Interesting."

"Why? Am I that far off the mark?"

"No. Closer than you could ever know, at least about the latter," she said with a regretful sigh.

He frowned. "Want to talk about it?"

"To you?"

"Why not? I'm here. I even have an entire pot of coffee we could share. It's a lot cheaper than a shrink."

She laughed at that. Suddenly feeling more daring than she had in years, she nodded. "Sure. Why not?"

He retrieved his jacket and tie, grabbed a cup from a neighboring table, poured them each a cup of coffee, then sat.

"So," he said, looking straight at her in a way that the two-timing Matthew hadn't dared for months. She liked that, liked the fact that this man didn't evade, liked that he was relaxed and unhurried, liked even more that he actually seemed interested in what she had to say. "Tell me why a beautiful woman like you is feeling lost. First though, tell me your name."

"Catherine," she said, feeling almost giddy with a shyness she hadn't experienced in a long time. Afternoon teas and charity balls had made her adept at small talk with strangers. Female strangers. Something about the man across from her suggested that inside where it counted he was no longer a stranger, that he was intuitively in tune with her, that he wanted to know her well. Best of all, he apparently saw her as a desirable woman and not as the eminent Dr. Matthew Devlin's cast-off wife.

"And the rest," he encouraged. "Who are you, Catherine, and why are you sitting here all alone?"

"I suppose if you wanted to drag out a cliché you could say that today is the first day of the rest of my life."

"You're getting a divorce."

She gave him a startled look.

He chuckled. "I'm not omniscient. You're tugging on your wedding band as though you can't quite make up your mind whether to take it off or leave it on. It's a dead giveaway."

She held out her hand and tried to examine the spectacular two-carat diamond and its simple wide gold setting with a certain amount of objectivity. She couldn't. She sighed as she admitted, "I hate what it represents, but I love the damn ring." She glanced at him ruefully. "Isn't it ridiculous to be so attached to a piece of jewelry?"

Instead of laughing tolerantly as Matthew would have, he took the question seriously. "It depends on why."

"Because we had it made to order from a stone that belonged to my great-grandmother. Nana Devereaux was a wonderful old lady. She was eighty-seven when she died. That was ten years ago and I still miss her."

"I think I understand, but don't you think it was a bad sign that your husband didn't buy you a new diamond?"

The criticism wasn't without merit, but Catherine found herself defending Matthew's choice. "Not at the time. I liked this one. It has sentimental value. Besides, he was just finishing a long surgical residency. I was barely twenty-one and just out of college. We were lucky he could afford the setting."

"Ah, the doctor syndrome. You nurtured him all through the lean years and then he ups and runs off with his nurse the minute the practice starts paying off."

"It was not his nurse," she retorted, just to remind this amazingly astute stranger that he didn't know *everything*.

"Oh?"

"It was a pediatrics resident."

He nodded and with obvious effort struggled to keep his impudent, know-it-all grin in check. "I'd forgotten about women's lib. What did she have that you don't have? I can't imagine anything."

"A career."

"And he found that attractive?"

"He found that convenient. Similar interests. Similar hours. And, I suppose, frequent opportunities to make it in the linen closets."

"And you're bitter."

"No," she admitted with mild astonishment. "I'm past bitter. I'm even past numb. Now I'm just frightened." The candor surprised her. She was not in the habit of revealing herself to anyone. Matthew had been a stickler for privacy, which had limited her friendships to mostly superficial ones. She found now that she'd missed the days of college confidences and shared intimacy. The man watching her so compassionately encouraged them, promised with gentle brown eyes to keep them private.

"I don't know where to go from here," she said. "What does a thirty-two-year-old woman do when she's on her own for the first time?"

"What have you been doing?"

"Raising money for a new pediatrics wing for the hospital." She couldn't keep the irony out of her tone.

"Hmm," he said with a solemnity that was mocked by the laughter in his eyes. "I can see why that might no longer appeal."

"I thought you might," she said wryly.

"Have you ever worked?"

"Try organizing a few luncheons for five hundred people and talking people out of a few thousand dollars. Believe me, that's work."

"But not the stuff of which résumés are built."

"Exactly," she said without the usual trace of defensiveness. "I have no idea what you do, but if you had a company, would you hire me?"

Apparently taking the question seriously, he looked her over very slowly. Catherine felt heat flooding her cheeks at the intense thoroughness of his survey. It was not entirely the cool, professional examination of a prospective employer. Her blood pulsed to a long-forgotten beat. "Maybe," he said finally.

She couldn't decide whether to be piqued by his caution or encouraged by his willingness to consider the possibility. "As what?"

"A model."

She burst out laughing. "Really, now. A man who can use a coffeepot to wrangle an introduction can surely come up with something more original than that."

"Don't laugh. You have nice bone structure, great skin and sexy, mysterious eyes. The camera would definitely love those eyes."

"Next thing I know you'll tell me you could make me a star."

"I probably could," he retorted so matter-of-factly that it gave her pause. "At least in commercials or print ads. I run an advertising agency in New York. I have a lot of accounts that could benefit from a spokeswoman with your obvious class." He glanced pointedly at the ring. "The diamond trade, for instance."

She turned her hand until the diamond glinted in the candlelight. "See. I told you it would come in handy. Why are you in Savannah? Are you scouting locations? This is a beautiful city."

"It is, but I'm just here to pursue a new account. We finished our meetings early, so I should have flown back. The last few months have been hell, though, so I decided to stay over a night." His gaze collided with hers, lingered. Her pulse raced wildly as he added in a seductive tone that promised unimaginable delights, "I'm glad I did."

"Me, too," she admitted quietly, shocking herself with the depth of her sincerity. After so many years of holding herself aloof, she found she was thriving on the unexpected intimacy, the sympathetic ear, the unthreatening banter with its faint hint of sensuality.

"Have you finished your dinner, Catherine?"

She stared down at the shrimp she'd barely touched and nodded. "I wasn't very hungry."

"Then let's get out of here and go for a walk along the river. Afterward, I'll buy you a nightcap."

The obligatory warnings screeched through her head. She peered deep into the stranger's eyes and saw nothing but honesty and compassion and the tiniest flame of desire. All drew her. All—even that carefully restrained suggestion of masculine interest— made the warnings seem unwarranted.

"If you can find my real waiter, so I can take care of my check, I'd love to join you for a walk," she said with an uncommonly bold sense of daring.

"I'll take care of it."

"No, really," she protested, thinking of her inbred sense of propriety.

"I won't take no for an answer. Someday you can return the favor when you see someone who looks lost and alone."

When the check had been paid, he guided her out of the crowded restaurant and across the cobbled street to the riverwalk. A soft, sultry breeze stirred the muggy air. A handful of glittering stars had been tossed across the velvet sky. The silence as they strolled was every bit as companionable as their conversation had been. With every step, though, the air of expectancy built. It pulsed and teased like the beat of a tango.

Unable to bear the mounting tension a moment longer, Catherine forced an innocent question. "You're not from here originally, are you?"

He glanced at her knowingly, obviously recognizing the query for what it was: a coward's step back from an unfamiliar closeness. "What was your first clue?" he taunted with a light acceptance of the diversion.

She laughed. "No drawl, for one thing."

"Any others?"

"You were eating dinner alone."

"Maybe I enjoy my own company."

"Maybe so, but I rather think a man like you could have the company of any number of women if you were on your home turf. A wife, for example?"

"Is that a leading question?"

She tilted her head up and smiled flirtatiously, even as she said, "It would only be a leading question if I were interested in you. Since we're just strangers passing in the night, it's simply a point of information."

"Ah, a fine distinction. As a man who knows the value of precise wording, I approve."

"You still haven't answered the question."

"Perhaps because, like you, thinking of my personal life is too painful."

"You're divorced?"

"In the process. My wife couldn't handle the amount of traveling I have to do, the impossible number of hours I have to put in."

"So she gave you an ultimatum?"

"Nope, no ultimatum. Just my walking papers. Apparently she didn't feel there was much point in discussing the obvious."

"The obvious being that you would choose work over her?"

"As she saw it."

"Was she right?"

His steps slowed and it was a long time before he answered. She had the feeling he was honestly soul-searching. "I wish I could say no," he said finally. "But I honestly don't know. I loved her and I miss our kids. That's the hardest part of all—knowing that I won't see them grow up, at least not the way I would living in the same house."

"Shouldn't you fight to get her back, then?"

"Would it be fair to do that if I couldn't keep the promise to change?"

"But you don't know that," she argued. "You haven't tried."

He sighed deeply. "No, I haven't tried. Maybe that says it all. When push came to shove, I didn't love her enough to try. She deserves much more than that. She's a terrific lady."

In the soft glow of the streetlight, Catherine saw the profound sadness and regret in his eyes. She wanted to reach out, to touch his cheek, but she held back. "At least you don't sound proud of walking away," she said.

"I'm not. If I could go back ten or fifteen years, maybe I'd do it all differently, but this is where I am today. I have to live with that."

"Isn't the trick to recognize where you are, decide if you like it and, if not, then make changes? That's what I'm trying to do. That's what brought me to Savannah. I'm looking for a new direction."

"Why here?"

"There's a school. It offers the kind of courses I once wanted very badly to take. They weren't really available when I was in college. In fact there's only one place in the country even now that offers a degree in historic preservation and it's here in Savannah."

"And?"

"I went by there today. Now I'm not so sure. Everyone seemed so young."

He opened his mouth, but she laughed and warned him, "Don't you dare tell me that age is only a state of mind."

"Ah, but it is, Catherine."

"Maybe so, but there's a season for everything and I think it's past time for me to be starting all over again as a college student."

"Don't give up so easily. Think how much knowledge and experience you'd take into a classroom. You'd be way ahead of your fellow students."

"I'd never thought of it quite like that. Thank you."

He stopped and turned her to face him. "Let's make a pact, you and I."

"Okay," she said, her serious tone matching his expression.

"Repeat after me, I do solemnly swear..."

"I do solemnly swear..."

"That I will spend the next year..."

"That I will spend the next year..."

"Discovering who I am and what I want out of life. No half measures, no rushing into things because of outside pressures."

Catherine felt a sigh building deep inside as she repeated the vow.

Her gaze met his. His eyes were filled with longing and regret as he lowered his head slowly until their lips barely met. His were soft as velvet as they brushed across her mouth. Then his arms slid around her waist, strong and possessive and loving. The kiss turned hungry and urgent, as feelings far too complicated swept through her, fulfilling earlier promises and altering forever the memory of their encounter. The innocence of it fled and in its place came a startling awareness, a powerful yearning to discover more of the taste and feel of him.

He finally pulled away, his hands lingering at her waist, his gaze searching her face. A faintly rueful smile tugged at his lips. "Ah, Catherine... if only things were different."

"If only... Two of the saddest words in all the language. Is that the way two people should live their lives?"

"Perhaps not. Shall we make another vow before I put you in a cab and send you off to your hotel?"

"Why not?" she said, fighting the sense of loss that was already stealing over her at the thought of their parting. A second loss—today of all days—was almost more than she could bear. Still, she managed a wavering smile.

"Do you remember the play about the couple who met just once a year and through the years came to know more about each other's lives than those who lived with them most intimately?''

*"Same Time, Next Year,"* she said at once. "I loved that play."

"Then let's make a promise to meet right here next year and see how our lives have changed."

"I'd like that," she said, entering into the fantasy of a time far in the future when things might be less complicated, when emotions might be less in turmoil. So much could happen in a year, so much could change. Just look at the past few months: her safe, predictable life had been turned topsy-turvy. She met his intense gaze and felt a slow heat begin to build deep inside. "I'd like that very much."

"Then I'll be waiting for you," he promised. "Coffeepot in hand." He stole one more kiss before whistling for a cab, tucking her inside and then walking away.

It wasn't until he was almost out of earshot that Catherine realized she didn't even know his name. With a sudden sense of urgency, she told the driver to stop, threw open the door and ran after him. At the sound of her footsteps on the cobblestones, he turned around. She halted in midstride, feeling suddenly foolish for wanting more, for needing that one link with someone she'd most likely never meet again, despite vows and best intentions.

"I don't even know your name," she explained with a helpless shrug. "I'd like to."

"Dillon," he replied, his voice so low she had to strain to catch the response.

"Dillon," she repeated. It fit somehow. Unique, thoroughly charming Dillon, an Irish rogue if ever she'd met one. She smiled with a serenity she hadn't felt in weeks and waved again as she got back into the taxi.

"Until next year," she whispered to herself as he disappeared from sight. It seemed as close as tomorrow.

And as far away as forever.

# One

---

"Catherine Devlin, what do you mean you're not going?" Beth Markham asked, her wide-eyed expression reflecting her amazement. "For the past twelve months all I've heard about is Dillon this and Dillon that."

"You're exaggerating. I haven't mentioned the man in ages." Catherine turned away to hide her embarrassment. With forced concentration she began piling the latest donations to St. Christopher's thrift shop onto the counter in front of her. She eyed the clothing critically, set the price and tagged each piece, hoping that Beth would go away or at least change the subject. Talking about Dillon made her nervous. So did, for that matter, remembering him. For a man she'd only talked with for a short time an entire year ago, a man she'd kissed just twice, he'd made an incredibly lasting impression.

"Last night," Beth said, sneaking up on her.

Catherine's black felt tip pen skittered wildly across the tag. Her heart hammered. "What?" she said as she ripped the ruined tag off and attached another one.

"You mentioned Dillon again last night."

"I did not." The denial was halfhearted. Though she hated admitting it, she suspected Beth knew exactly what she was talking about. She usually did. When it came to romance, Beth had the finely honed instincts of a successful matchmaker. Catherine was one of her few failures. Sensing that another meeting with Dillon could turn that around, Beth wasn't about to let Catherine off the hook.

"We were sitting at your kitchen table," Beth began, her amusement apparent. "I remember exactly how it happened. You started to take off your wedding ring. It's about time you did that, by the way. Anyway, then you said—and I quote—'Dillon said I could always be a model for the diamond trade.' And then you sighed."

"I did not," she repeated, only barely resisting the urge to sigh, thereby confirming Beth's smug statement.

"You did," Beth contradicted anyway. "You sigh every time you mention his name."

Catherine stopped tagging the clothes and turned slowly toward the woman who'd become her best friend over the last months when she'd been getting her feet back on the ground after the divorce. Beth was a delightful scatterbrain with a heart big enough to embrace the whole world. Though they'd been neighbors for years, it was only after Matthew had left that Catherine had gotten to know and appreciate her rare combination of wisdom, humor and blunt honestly.

"I do?" she said, dismayed by the sappy, love-struck picture of her that Beth was presenting. "I actually sigh?"

Beth nodded, grinning victoriously. "And you get this mysterious, faraway look in your eyes. You're smitten, Catherine Devlin, and I for one don't intend to listen to you going on and on about the man for the rest of your life. Today's the day you are supposed to meet him in Savannah. Now get out of here. It's a long drive and you'd better get started now if you intend to be there by dinnertime."

"I am not driving all the way to Savannah to meet a total stranger," she protested weakly.

"He's not exactly a stranger. Heck, I feel as if I know him by now."

Catherine glared at her. "I haven't been that bad."

"You have been, but don't worry. I think it's wonderfully romantic."

"You would." She shook her head. "No. It's ridiculous. It was a once-in-a-lifetime meeting. It's not the sort of thing you try to prolong." Despite the protest, the temptation to go, to take a risk for once, was gaining momentum.

Beth must have sensed her weakening. She pulled out her most powerful argument. "You made a vow, a solemn oath, didn't you? Are you going to go back on your word? Whatever would your mother say?" she drawled, deliberately mimicking the honey-thick Southern accent of Catherine's very proper mother.

"Don't drag her into this. If my mother knew I was even considering running off to Savannah to meet a man—a Northerner—I hardly know, she'd say plenty and it would blister your ears. I'd never hear the last of her disapproval. She barely tolerated Matthew because he'd only lived in Atlanta for a few years when we met."

"In the case of your ex-husband, she was right to be disapproving. The man was a self-righteous bore."

"He was not," she defended automatically, then realized that essentially she'd come to agree with Beth. Matthew had been a little stuffy, which had made that fling with the pediatrics resident all the more shocking. Maybe that had changed him, but the old Matthew would never in a million years have sanctioned exchanging polite chitchat with a total stranger, much less traipsing off to Savannah to meet a man she'd only known for a few hours. Still...

"Maybe..."

Beth seized on the hesitation with enthusiasm. "I knew it! You're going, aren't you? Now hurry up. You don't want to miss him."

"It's the middle of the week. The man does work, you know. He probably won't even be there."

"If he's not," Beth said practically, "you can go by the Savannah College of Art and Design again and check out the classes. It won't be a wasted trip."

"Don't start that again. I'm thirty-three. It's too late for me to take up a whole new career. I realized that when I was there last time."

"Fiddle-faddle! It's only too late when you're dead. Think about it, Cat. You're wasting yourself working in here. Not that I don't love having your help. I've actually had time off since you started volunteering, but you could do so much more."

"I'm happy now," she argued. "I have enough money to live on from the investments I made with the divorce settlement and with the trust fund from my father. What's wrong with just trying to make myself useful, giving something back to the community?"

"Nothing if it makes you happy, but it doesn't. I don't care what you say. You're going through the motions, filling up hours. Your year of mourning is up, sweetie. It's time to take some chances."

"Going to meet Dillon is about as much of a chance as I can cope with today."

"Then you'll go by the school tomorrow," Beth said with the persistence that had made her one of the best fund-raisers the church had ever had.

Catherine laughed. "Okay. You win. I promise I'll think about it."

She should have anticipated that wouldn't be quite good enough for Beth. "I'm going to ask to see catalogs and class schedules when you get back," Beth warned.

Catherine groaned. "No wonder your kids like to hide out at my house. You're a nag."

"If your house was littered with potato chips and socks, you'd nag, too."

"Maybe so," Catherine said, unable to keep a hint of unexpected wistfulness from her voice. At one time she'd wanted so badly to have children, but Matthew had been adamantly opposed. He liked to travel. He liked having her at his beck and call. And, though she could have defied him, she'd known that an "accidental" pregnancy was no answer. It would have created a horrible environment in which to bring up a child. The irony, of course, was that practically fifteen minutes after their divorce was final, Matthew had remarried because the pediatrics resident with whom he'd been having the affair was pregnant. Catherine figured it served him right.

"Maybe so," she said again, this time with more bitterness than she usually permitted herself.

Beth sobered at once, obviously reading the direction of her thoughts with her usual uncanny accuracy. "Don't look back, Cat. You can't change the past. Go out now and grab the future."

Catherine felt her heart begin to beat a little faster as the image of Dillon reappeared in her mind as it had so often over the past year. She recalled the way he'd listened to her, really listened, and the way he'd looked at her with such warmth and affection, as if they'd known each other forever.

"What the hell," she murmured finally. "You only live once."

All the way to Savannah, Catherine told herself she was a fool. Dillon wouldn't show up. Why would he?

He was an attractive man in a profession that threw him into contact with women far more beautiful, successful and sophisticated than she was. It had been an entire year. Just because she hadn't been able to get him out of her mind didn't mean he would remember their few hours together or the promise they'd made.

No matter how determinedly she tried to balance her excitement with a healthy dose of reality, though, the anticipation was winning. She'd had a lot of dates during the past year, but none had filled her with this pins-and-needles expectancy. In fact, she only dimly remembered feeling this way with Matthew during the first heady days of their courtship fifteen years earlier, when she'd just started college and he'd been in medical school. Recalling that reminded her how fleeting such emotions could be.

But even that sobering reminder wasn't able to dampen her sense of adventure six hours later as she dressed in a simple red dress that flattered her dark coloring. She added gold jewelry and a subtle touch of her favorite perfume, a French floral scent that Matthew had hated, probably because she'd paid a hundred dollars an ounce for it. Sliding her feet into a pair of very high black heels that made her look sinfully wicked, she left for the restaurant, which was only a few blocks away on the waterfront.

It was a balmy night with only the faintest breeze stirring off the river. As she walked, she recalled that slight flaring of desire she'd seen in Dillon's eyes before he'd kissed her and said goodbye. Her pulse throbbed at the thought of his lips on hers again—warm, sensuous, demanding. An aching heaviness low in her abdomen told her once more just how captivated she'd been, how much she wanted him to be waiting for her tonight.

At the restaurant door, she hesitated, stricken with a sudden shyness, a sudden onset of sanity. Was she crazy for coming? Was she taking an incredible risk? The news was filled with such horrible stories.... The memory of Dillon's gentle kindness allayed her fears. She caught her reflection in the restaurant window and saw the slow curve of her mouth. "Don't back out now, Cat," she murmured and slipped inside before she could change her mind.

She quickly scanned the dimly lit room. It was early yet and there were only a few customers. There was no sign of a familiar man in a designer suit, looking as if he'd just stepped out of the pages of some elite men's magazine. Her gaze slid to the table where she'd been sitting when they met. It was available. She asked the hostess if she could be seated there.

Once she was sitting down, she realized that her hands were trembling. She hadn't been this nervous on her very first date. She'd never been this afraid of being stood up. She ordered a glass of white wine and the shrimp, the same meal she'd had a year earlier. For luck, she told herself.

"More coffee?" The seductive masculine voice sent a jolt of pure electricity sizzling down her spine.

"I'm not drinking coffee," she said in a voice that went breathless in midsentence. She looked up into serious brown eyes that studied her with relentless intensity.

"You came," she said softly, fighting to hide the sigh of relief that whispered through her.

Dillon's smile seemed to hold a similar measure of satisfaction. "So did you."

"I didn't think you'd remember," they said together, then laughed. The laughter broke the tension and made Catherine delightfully aware that she'd never wanted to be anyplace more than where she was right now with this handsome, kind man regarding her with such obvious warmth.

"You look wonderful," he said as he sat down, his appreciation evident in eyes that caressed, paying loving attention to every detail from head to toe. Catherine's skin burned under the intense scrutiny. "I'm sorry I'm late."

"You're not. I mean we really didn't set a time exactly. I wasn't even sure if you'd bother to come all this way for a dinner. Or did you get that account down here? Do you come often now?" She had to bite her tongue to stop the nervous rattling off of questions.

"Yes, I got the account and I do come down occasionally. I made it a point to be here tonight. I was hoping that you'd remember, that you'd want to see me again. I can't tell you how many times in the last year I've regretted not getting your last name, not being able to call you to see how you were doing."

She regarded him curiously. "I've felt the same way," she admitted with unfamiliar boldness. "Why didn't you ask for the phone number?"

His expression turned thoughtful. "I suppose it was because we were both at a low point in our lives that night. We were both reaching out for something that, amazingly enough, we each had to offer, but that's a dangerous time to start something. For once in my life I listened to my conscience, instead of rushing into something. I knew in my gut that we needed time to sort out our lives. I took a risk and turned things over to fate."

This once, then, the Fates had proved kind. Generous, in fact. She propped her chin in her hand and asked, "And did you sort out your life?"

"As best I could. The divorce is final. I'm working on building a better relationship with my children. Ironically, I seem to spend more time with them now than I did when I was married, maybe because I make the time. I've stopped taking them for granted."

"Ah, yes, one of life's greatest sins, taking those we love for granted."

"What about you? Have you sorted things out?"

"I've survived. I'm learning to rely on myself. I'm building an identity that's separate from being Dr. Matthew Devlin's wife. I don't have it entirely together yet, but I'm trying."

"Is there a man helping you to find your way?" he asked. Catherine thought she heard a note of caution in his voice, an unexpected tentativeness.

"No," she said adamantly, drawing a broad smile. "This time I thought it wise to find my own way, to discover who I really am and then see if a man fits into that picture, instead of the other way around."

"See," he teased, "it is possible to learn from our mistakes."

Catherine found herself smiling back at him. She was slowly relaxing, falling under the magical spell of his interest all over again, wanting to share things with him that she'd never shared with anyone, not even Beth. "It seems to me we've both paid quite a price to learn that lesson."

"Ah, but we're much better people now. Think how good we'll be to each other."

The low, seductive taunt set off a fire in her belly. She wanted to look away, but his gaze held her, demanded that she acknowledge the desire that was building so quickly between them, a longing so intense that it made her weak. He took her hand in his, rubbing her knuckles with the pad of his thumb.

"I can't believe how I've missed you," he said softly. "How is it possible that two people could connect so easily after one brief meeting?"

"Are you certain it's not just wishful thinking?" she asked shakily, clinging to reality even as it seemed to be falling away, leaving her senses raw and vulnerable.

"I'm not certain of anything, but I do know that if you hadn't been here tonight, I would have moved heaven and earth to find you. I would have come after you sooner, but I forced myself to keep my word, to wait a year. Even so, there wasn't a trip to Savannah that I didn't stop by here hoping to catch a glimpse of you again, not a moment that I didn't look at every tall, dark beauty to see if she might be you. There were so many things I wanted to talk over with you, so many times I've wondered what you'd think about an ad campaign I was creating or a play I was seeing or a book I was reading."

"But why?" she asked, bemused by the passionate declaration. "Why would you want the opinion of someone you barely knew?"

He shrugged ruefully. "I wish I understood that. I know all about the psychology of advertising, all about titillating the public, but I don't understand what's going on between us. There was just something about that night, an overwhelming intuition. I knew at once that you and I were on the same wavelength, that what we had was too special to lose. You must have felt it, too, or you wouldn't be here now."

Catherine was shaken by how closely his feelings matched hers. "I suppose I did," she admitted finally. "Beth—she's a neighbor I've grown close to this last year—says I'm still quoting you after all this time." She flushed. "I probably shouldn't tell you that."

"Why not? I just told you how I felt."

"But women are supposed to be coy. Don't you know that in the South at least it's something we're trained to do from the cradle on? My mother would be horrified if she knew I was giving away my feelings like this. Frankly, I'm a little surprised at myself."

"Why?"

"Because I've always been so cool and reserved, not just coy, mind you, but private. For some reason I open up with you."

"Because you know I'd never hurt you."

She stared at him and thought about his statement. It could have been nothing more than glib charm, but she believed it was true. She knew in her heart that Dillon would do anything in his power to keep from hurting her, that he was a gentle, compassionate man. And she was responding to that knowledge like a flower opening to sunshine.

That didn't mean the feelings didn't confuse her. "How do I know that?" she wondered.

"You have superb instincts," he suggested lightly.

"I chose Matthew," she reminded him.

"Maybe it's my honest face, then."

"You have the face of a heartbreaker."

"Then maybe it's magic."

"Or illusion."

"Cynic."

"Realist," she countered, laughing at his crestfallen expression.

"We are going to have a wonderful time finding out, though, aren't we, Catherine?"

"Yes," she said quietly, folding her fingers around his. "Yes, I think we are."

For the first time in years, something other than work was on Dillon's mind the instant he woke up. Catherine! The memory of the trusting way she'd looked at him last night, the delight that had come over her fragile features when he'd appeared at her table, the yearning he'd recognized when he'd left her at the door of her hotel room at 1:00 a.m. with one sweet, lingering kiss. He'd wanted so much more, but he'd sworn to move slowly with her, to take the time to treasure these rare new feelings that were bursting within him. Restraint was far from a habit for him and he was just now discovering it was the pits. His whole body ached from the effort.

Though his actions had been restrained, he hadn't minced words. He'd told her the absolute truth. Not a day had gone by in the past year, when she hadn't crossed his mind, when he hadn't recalled her combination of sophisticated looks and gentle vulnerability. He'd wanted to explore her quick intelligence just as much as he'd wanted to savor her incredible body. The fact that he'd given her mind precedence over her sensuality told him exactly how far-gone he was. From the very first, he'd known that she was going to be someone important in his life, someone to respect and cherish, not use and discard. Thank heavens for once he'd listened to his conscience.

Right now, though, he was damning it. He was lying in bed, aching with the need to touch her. Aching was the operative word, too. It was not the first time that thoughts of Catherine had driven him into an icy shower. This morning though, he would be seeing her again, albeit far too briefly. He had a noon flight back to New York to make a three o'clock meeting that couldn't be postponed. He'd had to rearrange half a dozen appointments to get here at all, but it would have taken a collapse of the airline industry and the force of a hurricane to keep him away from Savannah last night. He'd spent three hundred and sixty-five days dreaming of holding her in his arms again.

He reached over, picked up the phone and dialed her room. "Wake up, sleepyhead," he said cheerfully.

"It's early," she murmured in a whispery voice that set his blood on fire all over again.

"We only have a few hours. Let's not waste them. Breakfast in twenty minutes. I'll pick you up."

"An hour," she bargained.

"Thirty minutes and not a second more." He hung up on her protest.

She met him at the door of her room, still barefooted and with her long, dark hair curling damply about her perfect, just-scrubbed face. If anything, she was even more beautiful without makeup. She smelled of soap and lavender. If he'd recognized the product he would have offered to write an entire ad campaign for free. The scent was heady, deliciously provocative, yet innocent of artifice.

"You're early," she accused.

"I'm right on time."

"I'm not ready."

"You look beautiful."

"I look wet."

He brushed a damp tendril back from her face and watched the heat flare in her blue eyes. "Beautiful," he said huskily, claiming her lips. They were morning soft and mint-scented moist. He wanted to taste them for hours, to discover the shape and texture at every stage of arousal. He let her go on a ragged moan. It took all of his strength to resist the urge to demand more, to release her when he felt her body molding itself to his.

"You're dangerous, lady."

Surprised pleasure registered on her face. "Me?"

"Yes, you. Have you no idea how tempting you are?"

"No."

The honest admission made his heart flip over. What a glorious feeling it would be to show this woman exactly how desirable she was, to tap her passions in a way he suspected her ex-husband had ignored. *Not now,* he warned himself. As badly as he wanted her, as convinced as he was that she wanted him, he wasn't going to rush her and scare her to death. She might enjoy their passion, she might come to life under his touches, but she wouldn't thank him for it. She reminded him of an orchid, hothouse sultry, but fragile.

"Hurry," he said, sending her off to dry her hair. "I'm a hungry man."

A short time later, Catherine picked daintily at her breakfast of dry toast and half a grapefruit, while he wolfed down eggs, bacon, grits and toast, then wondered about the blueberry muffins.

"Surely not," she said, her eyes widening incredulously.

"Just one. You can share it with me."

He placed the order and when the huge muffin came, he broke off bits, buttered them and fed them to her. He talked of his meeting in New York, keeping her attention diverted from the food she was accepting. She'd finished the whole muffin before she realized that he hadn't had a single bite. "You tricked me," she said.

"How did I do that?" he asked innocently.

"You didn't want that muffin at all."

"But you obviously did."

She studied him with apparent astonishment. "How did you know?"

His expression sobered as he took her hand, slowly licking the last crumbs of muffin from her fingertips. The pulse that beat in her neck leaped at his touch. "I know everything about you."

"Oh?"

"Well, maybe not everything, but what I don't know now, I will soon."

"Soon?"

"I've been thinking."

"Why do I think that's a dangerous precedent?"

He scowled at her. "Memorial Day is coming up. Could you get away and meet me here again? We'd have the whole weekend then to explore the area, to get to know each other."

She hesitated and his heart seemed to stand still. "Maybe we're trying to turn this into something it isn't," she responded cautiously.

"And maybe we're not. How will we know unless we explore the possibilities? Are you willing to walk away again without trying?"

"No," she said finally, then lifted her gaze to collide with his. Her chin rose almost imperceptibly. "No, I'm not."

Dillon grinned. "One week from tomorrow then. Same time. Same place."

She nodded slowly. "Same time. Same place."

# Two

---

*Memorial Day Weekend*

**D**illon's plane was late. An impatient man under the best of circumstances, today he was infuriated by the delay. He paced. He cursed the airline. He cursed the cluttered skies over New York. He cursed himself for having sold his private jet. And while he was at it, he cursed Catherine for so quickly becoming an obsession. From that very first meeting he'd known that she was capable of driving him mad with longing. Still, he hadn't been able to resist her.

In fact, had it not been for Catherine, he'd never have made the rash decision to take the Savannah account in the first place. Every finely honed business instinct had told him to turn it down. White Stone Electronics was a small company and though the potential was great, it could be years before the account became really profitable for him. Yet, during those brief hours he'd spent with Catherine, he'd known he was going to accept, known he was going to grab the excuse to return to the city where they'd met, to cling to the one link between them.

Oddly, the small account had become the most satisfying he'd handled in years. Most of the *Fortune 500* firms with which he worked didn't really need his help. They wanted catchy ads to maintain an already high profile or a public service program to enhance an already established image. This company had no national reputation, except among a few discerning clients. It needed everything, and the results, the sudden spurts of growth that had followed the first ads had been gratifying in ways he'd almost forgotten.

Even so, even though he'd proven that his faith in the company was justified, no one in the New York headquarters of his agency could understand his continued involvement, much less the all-too-frequent trips to Savannah. After the first few years in business, his role had been to land the most illustrious new accounts, set the direction of campaigns and keep the major clients happy. As a result, it had been years since he'd experienced the satisfaction of seeing one of his own creations move from conception to television screens or the pages of a slick magazine. In the past few months he'd found himself reliving the gut-level kick of hearing people on the subway or in the supermarket talk about one of his commercials.

For the past few months, he'd found himself increasingly anxious to get back to Savannah where his creative juices flowed more freely than ever before. Today, though, his impatience was caused by something else entirely.

Catherine.

Since he'd left her this last time, he hadn't been able to get her out of his mind. If the memories had tantalized him during that long year apart, the past week or so had been sheer torture. She was in his blood, heating it in a way that no woman had in years. With her pale-as-cream complexion, those huge vulnerable blue eyes and that regal aura of self-containment that taunted a man, she was a delightful challenge. He'd said it all when he'd told her she had class. To a kid from his poor background, a man who'd struggled for every single success that had dragged him from a lousy neighborhood to the Upper East Side, she represented the unattainable, the sort of woman to be put on a pedestal. She was a dream for him, but she was also flesh-and-blood real.

A dozen times he'd picked up the phone to call, but held back. Sensing her skittishness, he hadn't wanted to pressure her. Or maybe he'd simply panicked, fearing the rapid deepening of his own involvement. Suddenly, after discovering that her hold over his senses hadn't diminished, maybe he was running scared, maybe that—not sheer lust—explained the way his pulse quickened at the thought of her. However strong the fear though, he hadn't been even remotely tempted not to fly down to meet her tonight. If the plane didn't take off in the next ten minutes, he was going to change airlines, charter a jet, whatever it took to get him there.

Two hours later, when he finally walked off the plane and saw her waiting for him, his heart caught, then hammered. Hanging back for just an instant, he saw her anxious eyes scanning the arriving passengers. As the exodus dwindled down, her high brow furrowed in a slight frown. Unable to hide in the shadows a moment longer, Dillon began striding toward her. When she caught sight of him, the worried frown vanished, replaced by a dazzling, heart-stopping smile of welcome. The warmth in her eyes, the childlike spark of anticipation set his blood on fire all over again. He was hooked all right. No man could inspire a look like that without feeling a fierce swell of possessiveness, a sudden yearning for the sort of passion that was all-too-elusive in life. Matthew Devlin must have been a first-class fool to let her get away.

Dillon reached out and took her hands. Hungry for a kiss, for the feel of her lips crushed beneath his, he satisfied himself with the amazingly shy, trusting clasp of her fingers around his.

"Sorry I'm late."

She tilted her head inquiringly, revealing a flash of the finest gold on her delicately shaped ears. "Were you flying the plane?"

Grinning at the teasing question, he shook his head.

"Then there's no reason to apologize, is there? Besides, do you have any idea how fascinating an airport can be?"

"Frankly, no."

"Interested in a tour? There's a lovely newsstand and the coffee shop has a waitress who must have come from New York. She'd make you homesick, she's so rude. It reminded me of a deli I went into once in midtown Manhattan. The nastiest waitresses seemed to get the biggest tips. Why is that? You all not only put up with it, you actually encourage it."

"Maybe because their regulars know they can count on them to be there day in and day out, never changing. Constancy is something to be treasured, especially in a city as quick to change as New York."

She looked doubtful.

"Okay," he said. "You don't buy that. Maybe it's just because it gives us somebody we can justify yelling back at before we've had our morning coffee. If we snap at a waitress, she'll punish us with cold coffee. If we snap at our wives, they'll divorce us and take us to the cleaners in the process."

"That sounds more like it. What about you? Are you a morning person?"

"Actually, I am. I never snapped at Paula over breakfast. I'd usually left the house long before she even got up. And I never growl at waitresses. Do you really want to stand here talking about my temper in the morning?"

"Actually, yes," she said.

Puzzled, he glanced into her too-serious eyes. "Why?"

Her aristocratic chin lifted with the faintest suggestion of defiance. Once again he spotted that astounding vulnerability and the stubborn determination to overcome it. "Because a part of me is terrified of what comes next," she admitted.

"Nothing that you don't want," he promised, touched by her determined honesty and awed by the suggestion of innocence in a woman who should have been filled with self-assurance. He recognized once more that such personal revelations were rare for her, something to be treasured and encouraged.

"Even if I have to spend the entire weekend in an icy shower," he added wryly.

"Maybe my mother would overlook your Northern beginnings after all," she said thoughtfully, a teasing glint lighting her blue eyes. "You have definitely captured the spirit of a Southern gentleman."

The praise was a mixed blessing. "Let's just hope my weak flesh can live up to my willing spirit," he said.

"I have every confidence in you," she said, linking her arm through his and playing havoc with his honorable intentions.

"I know," he said, barely containing a sigh of pure pleasure at her touch. "That's what makes it so damned difficult. If I ever succumbed to a moment of intense passion, I'd feel guilty about it for the rest of my life. Now let's stop talking about this. Have you decided where you'd like to go for dinner?"

"The same place. I feel as though it's lucky for us."

"You're superstitious?"

"Just hedging my bets. Do you mind?"

"Not at all, as long as you don't expect me to serve the coffee. Last time the people at the next table complained because I didn't pour for them."

Catherine's lilting laughter, suddenly carefree and unrestrained, filled the air. Dillon felt as though she'd bestowed a precious gift on him.

The restaurant was packed to capacity with holiday weekend visitors to Savannah, but the hostess took one look at Dillon and promised to do what she could. They were seated within minutes. The dinner was the best yet. Catherine actually tasted the shrimp for the first time and savored the spicy seasonings.

"This is terrific," she said with unconcealed astonishment.

"It's the third time you've had it," Dillon pointed out.

"But it's the first time I was paying any attention." She regarded him intently. "You actually remember what I had over a year ago on the night we met?"

"I remember everything about that night," he said and her heart thumped unsteadily. He placed his hand on the table, palm up, and after only the tiniest hesitation she linked her fingers through his. The contact sent shivers racing along her spine. His hot, hungry gaze melted her resolve to move ahead slowly, to keep him at arm's distance until she really knew him.

"Dillon, you promised," she accused in a breathless voice.

He stared back innocently. "I'm not doing a thing."

"You are," she insisted, drawing back her hand. Even without his touch, though, her pulse didn't quiet and her flesh didn't cool. She folded her hands tightly together in her lap and sat up straighter. "Tell me about your week."

His low chuckle washed over her, teasing at her senses and making mincemeat of her attempt to regain control over her rampaging hormones. "I made a few bucks. How about you?"

She ignored the flip reply. She'd pursue the details about his week later. "I worked at the shop and went to three tedious luncheons for very good causes," she said just as glibly. "I'd rather have sent them the money."

"Why didn't you?"

"Because they tell me that listing my name on the committee helps to raise more money. What it really means is I feel guilty unless I get on the phone and insist that my friends turn out. Then I have to do the same for their charities. Pretty soon I'm up to my eyeballs in chicken salad and fresh raspberries."

"You said something about calling the College of Art and Design this week to make an appointment. Did you? I'd like to go by and take a look at the place. I've heard a lot more about it since I've been coming down here regularly."

Despite Dillon's apparent interest, Catherine immediately felt defensive. "You sound like Beth," she grumbled lightly. "Please, don't you turn into a nag, too. I'll get to it one of these days."

"It's not too soon to check out fall classes," he persisted with the determination of a man not used to wasting time. "If you were living in Savannah, we could see even more of each other."

He held out the possibility of more time together like a delightful temptation, but it came with strings. She wasn't prepared to make a change so drastic in her life-style, not for any man, especially when she wasn't ready to do it for herself.

"Can't we table this conversation?" she pleaded.

He seemed genuinely confused by her hesitation. She envied his self-assurance, his quick decision-making skill. Dillon was obviously a man who always grabbed for the brass ring, relishing the success, but willing to risk the defeats. She wasn't nearly so brave. Yet, she amended. She was getting stronger by the day.

"Why don't you want to discuss it?" he asked.

She took a deep breath and admitted, "Because every time one of you brings it up, I start to feel like a failure."

Dillon looked stunned at her heartfelt candor. "A failure? This isn't about failing, Catherine. I thought working in historic preservation was something you wanted. I'm just trying to encourage you."

"I mentioned it a couple of times. What you and Beth are doing feels more like pressure than encouragement."

"Because you're scared," he said with another of those uncanny flashes of intuition. "Is that it?"

"Damn right, I'm scared," she retorted. "I'm leading a safe, secure life right now. Why should I turn it upside down on some whim?"

"If that's all it is, then you're right." He studied her intently. "Is it just a whim?"

Catherine sighed. "I don't know anymore. Every time I walk through this town and see how much has been accomplished, I get excited all over again. Then I go home and fall back into a familiar routine and I don't see the point. There are plenty of other people to tackle preservation projects. The school's reputation is growing. The work is exciting. It's new. The country is finally beginning to see the importance of preserving history, instead of knocking it down and replacing it with another high rise. Savannah's been a leader in that fight."

"Things may be changing here. People in Savannah do have a genuine commitment, but there aren't that many leaders for the fight yet in other cities. How many historic buildings in Atlanta fell so they could build the new downtown stadium? That's right in your own backyard."

Catherine cringed at the accuracy of the charge. She'd spoken out, but she hadn't actually led a crusade. She hadn't been in there pitching alternatives. Maybe she was just one of those people who was committed to a cause only as long as it was easy, only as long as the main requirements were cash and time, not the risk of controversy.

"You're right," she said miserably. "I walked away from a fight. Maybe that's the worst carryover from my marriage. I've forgotten how to stand up for myself and what I believe in. I spent too many years focused totally on Matthew's goals and one of his primary objectives in life was to avoid controversy."

"It doesn't have to be that way, you know. You're too intelligent and caring to take the easy way out forever."

She grabbed at the praise like a lifeline. "What makes you so confident of that?"

"I see the spirit in your eyes, the flashes of temper. You bank them before they get out of hand, but they're there. Yelling back just takes a little practice."

Suddenly she realized just how often she did bite her tongue to avoid making a scene, how often she kept her opinions to herself in the name of diplomacy. Matthew had prized her tact and her even temper almost more highly than her knack for choosing the best wine and creating the most extravagant entrées. "Be careful," she warned Dillon. "You may be creating a monster. The next thing you know you won't be able to utter a word without me challenging you."

He grinned. "I'm a born street fighter, sweetheart. I'll take my chances. Now finish that wine and let's get out of here. There's someplace I think we should go."

"Where?"

"You'll see," he said mysteriously. No matter how hard she prodded, he wouldn't reveal his plans.

It was just as well. When they left the restaurant, the waterfront was alive with holiday weekend activity. There was a concert in progress and the crowds from each of the restaurants and clubs spilled out onto the riverwalk. Some paused to listen to the music. Others strolled at a leisurely pace, pursued by the sultry strains of jazz.

"Stay or go?" Dillon asked, watching her face.

The beat of the music came alive inside her, tugging at her heart. "Stay," she said at once as flute and trumpet soared with impossible beauty and clarity.

Dillon found a spot to stand, where they could hear the music and see the shadowy forms on the river. Leaning back against the low wall, he pulled her back against him, his arms linked around her midriff. The heat of his body surrounded her, the press of his hard, muscled thighs tempted. Every fiber of her being from head to toe was vibrantly aware of him, filled with the musky, masculine scent of him. Her breasts ached from the longing to be touched. She folded her arms around her middle, her hands atop Dillon's. It took every ounce of restraint she possessed to keep from lifting those strong fingers just inches higher to caress and tease. His warm breath whispered past her ear and Catherine felt a sigh shudder through her.

"Look up," he said in a hushed, awestruck voice. "Quickly."

She glanced at the sky.

"A falling star," he said, pointing. "Make a wish."

Savoring the unexpectedly powerful feeling of contentment that being in his arms brought, she told him honestly, "I don't think I could wish for anything more than this."

Catherine awoke to the sound of impatient knocking and Dillon's voice.

"Rise and shine, my long-stemmed beauty!"

Laughing, she drew on her robe and opened the door. "Long-stemmed beauty?"

"Isn't there some poem about a love that's like a red rose? That's how I think of you. You're as elegant and petal-soft as an American Beauty rose. For a bit I thought you were more like an orchid, but last night I began to detect the strength, the thorns."

"Thanks...I think. Do you always go on so poetically at—" she glanced at her bedside clock "—barely 9:00 a.m.?"

"I rarely have the inspiration," he admitted. "Do you want your breakfast on the table over there or in bed?"

"That depends," she said cautiously. "Are you sharing it with me?"

"Absolutely."

"Then you'd better put it on the table."

He sighed dramatically. "I was afraid you were going to say that."

"What did you bring?" she asked, realizing that she was starved. Maybe Dillon wasn't going to be good for her after all. Now that she had her appetite back in his presence, she had a feeling she could puff up like a pastry in no time if she didn't watch herself.

As if he could read her mind, he taunted, "No dieting allowed this weekend. You'll eat everything on your plate."

"Now you sound just like the family housekeeper. My mother's grapefruit breakfasts and my half-grapefruit and dry toast made her crazy. When my father had to give up eggs, Maisie almost retired. She said there wasn't any point to knowing how to cook if nobody in the house was going to eat a blasted thing. She threatened to put out bowls of birdseed and be done with it.''

"Did she do it?''

"Of course not. Maisie would die if she didn't have my parents to boss around. Her biggest regret is that she only gets to bully me at Sunday dinners now. I can't bear the look on her face when I turn down dessert. Are you ever going to open those bags or am I going to have to steal them from you?''

"That could be interesting,'' Dillon said, lifting the two huge white sacks just beyond her reach. She stood on tiptoe and stretched. His laughing gaze locked with hers, then drifted slowly down, turning hot and leaving fire and breathless anticipation in its wake. As his burning gaze lingered on her chest, Catherine realized that her robe was coming loose, leaving only the faintest scrap of lace to cover her breasts from Dillon's intent examination.

"Catherine...'' he began, his voice suddenly hoarse.

Her own breath had lodged in her throat and her heart hammered in her chest. "Yes,'' she whispered.

"I...'' He cleared his throat, then shook his head as if coming out of a trance. "I think we'd better eat.''

She nodded weakly and sat down hurriedly, tugging her robe more tightly around her and belting it securely.

Opening the bag with fingers that trembled, Dillon removed croissants that were still warm from the oven, containers of homemade jam, cups of fresh chilled melon, real silverware borrowed from the inn's dining room and huge cups of steaming coffee. Reaching back in the bag one more time, he extracted a thick pamphlet and placed it in front of Catherine. She recognized the logo of the College of Art and Design and suddenly her appetite vanished.

"Dillon, you're pressing."

"It wouldn't hurt to look it over, would it? I thought we could stop by later and talk to someone over there about fall enrollment."

Catherine began to feel as if she was battling a steamroller. And losing. "Why is it so important to you that I do this?"

"It's not important to me that you do this. It's important for you."

"How can you say that? You don't even know me. You latched onto one little thing I said and you're turning it into a cause."

"Hardly that," he said, calmly putting jam on his croissant. Catherine felt like shaking him for being so disgustingly in control. Despite her fierce scowl, he kept on. "You did tell me this was something you'd once wanted badly. You keep saying you're bored with all those luncheons. As far as I can tell the only thing keeping you from enrolling in this program is the age thing. I just want you to see how silly that is. Now do you still think I don't know you?"

"Okay, superficially, maybe," she admitted grudgingly, not willing to concede any more than that. "That doesn't give you the right to interfere in my life, to take the decision out of my hands."

"Is it interfering to want what's best for you?"

"Not if I get to choose what's best."

"Then choose, Catherine. Make a choice. Any choice. I'll back you up."

There was an odd note of censure in his tone that infuriated her. He had no right, none at all, to suggest that what she was doing with her life now wasn't enough. She threw down her napkin and stood up. "Maybe this is a mistake, Dillon. Maybe we should have left well enough alone."

He seemed to go perfectly still. "Meaning?" he said very quietly.

She began to pace, glaring at him for ruining what had seemed so perfect only twenty-four hours earlier. "That some fantasies don't hold up all that well under closer scrutiny. You're every bit as domineering in your way as Matthew was in his. I won't let another man run my life. I don't want to be molded into your version of the ideal woman."

"Hey, slow down. I don't want to run your life. I want you to do it. There's a big difference."

"I am running my life."

"Are you really? I don't see it."

"That's because you're obsessed with your career. You think everyone who isn't a workaholic is bored."

"I don't give a good damn whether or not you have a career," he retorted with obvious impatience. "Can you honestly tell me you were totally happy being a housewife? Did that satisfy you? Were you content with running a house and doing good deeds?"

The harsh words hammered at her. "No, dammit," she exploded finally, shocked by the anger that was racing through her like a heady wine. She was shaking with years of pent-up fury. "I hated it. I deplored the sameness of it, but it was expected of me and I was good at it."

Surprisingly, Dillon heaved a sigh of relief at the explosion. "I'm sure you were," he said more gently and Catherine felt the anger begin to ebb. "I think you'd be good at whatever you did."

She turned tear-filled eyes to meet his as he added, "This time, though, make it something that means something to you, something important, something your very soul needs to feel fulfilled."

Suddenly it dawned on her what he'd done. She wasn't sure which irritated her more, that he'd tried it or that it had worked. "You made me fight with you on purpose, didn't you?" she said suspiciously.

"Maybe."

"Don't try to manipulate me again, Dillon," she said seriously. A new strength seemed to fill her. She probably should thank him for that, but she didn't. She warned instead, "You might win the battle, but I guarantee you'll lose the war."

Rather than looking one bit intimidated, he looked pleased. "Deal," he said.

Unconvinced by the sudden reversal of tactics, she stared into brown eyes that never once wavered. Finally, she nodded and sank back into her chair. She took a long, grateful sip of coffee. Her voice calmer, she asked, "Is that the way advertising is for you? Would you feel empty without it?"

"Sometimes," he said with surprising caution.

"I thought you loved it. Every time you talk about White Stone Electronics you get this spark in your eye, like you can't wait to get back to it. I was envious of that. I want something I care about that much."

"White Stone has made me see how much I've lost by becoming a success."

"Isn't that a contradiction?"

"I don't think so. Not if being a success takes you away from the part of the job you love the most. It's like a teacher who adores working with students suddenly being tapped to be principal. That's success. He's still an educator. But he's no longer in the classroom."

"What does that mean for you?"

"I'm not sure yet. Maybe, like you, I'll find the answers here in Savannah. Are you game?"

With a deeply indrawn breath, she finally nodded. "Where do we start?"

"Let's visit that school. We'll take the rest one step at a time." At her doubtful look, he emphasized, "Both of us."

"Sure," she said at last. "What have I got to lose? A job in a thrift shop that doesn't pay, has no fringe benefits and could be done by any able-bodied adult with a speck of sense. Almost anything would be better than that, right?"

"That's the right attitude," he said approvingly.

"Spunky?" she said with apparent distaste.

Dillon chuckled. "Definitely spunky." He picked up her hand and kissed the palm. "Sexy, too."

The lightest touch of his lips generated the force of an earthquake. Catherine felt the tremor clear down to her toes. Maybe spunky was going to turn out to be all right, after all, she thought as she met Dillon's bold, heated gaze. He winked slowly and her pulse quickened.

Then again, she decided with equal parts regret and anticipation, it was probably just going to get her into trouble.

# Three
___

*Fourth of July*

"**W**hat's this?" Beth asked with feigned innocence as she picked up the sheer negligee tossed on Catherine's bed.

Catherine snatched it back. "What does it look like?"

"Pure seduction." Beth settled herself on the bed and turned a curious gaze on Catherine. "Tell me again about this weekend. What does Dillon have in mind?"

"He's rented a cottage at Hilton Head."

"Well, well," she said with gloating approval. "I take it things are working out."

Catherine glared at her friend. "He's a nice man," she declared defensively.

"Did I suggest otherwise? Even if I had, you certainly don't have to justify yourself to me."

"That's right." Noting Beth's increasingly amused expression, Catherine sighed and sank down on the edge of the bed beside her, twisting the sheer negligee fabric into knots. "I sound so self-confident. Why do I feel as though I'm still a teenager sneaking around behind my parents' backs?"

"Because you haven't mentioned Dillon to your mother," Beth said at once. "Why does that bother you so much? You're way past the age when you should have to account to anyone other than yourself for your actions."

"I know that, but mother is hurt that I won't be spending the holiday with the whole family while they're in North Carolina. She's also convinced that I'm going to sit around here by myself moping. You know how she feels about that sort of self-indulgence."

"Then tell her the truth. Tell her moping is the last thing on your mind these days."

"Beth!"

"Well, it's the truth, isn't it? You're the happiest I've seen you. Maybe it would be good for her to know that there's a new man in your life. She'd stop worrying so much."

"You've got to be kidding. My mother has turned worrying into a full-time profession. No, if I tell her, she'll just ruin it for me. You've seen her in action. She'll have Dad investigating Dillon's credit rating. Then she'll call him herself and invite him to Atlanta for a full-dress inspection. I'm not ready to face all that. I doubt Dillon is, either. He's not the kind of man who'll enjoy being trotted out for a stamp of approval like a hunk of meat."

"Don't you think he'll measure up? From everything you said this man could pass a government security check and the judging for hunk-of-the-month."

"Mother's standards are higher. Even so, Dillon could meet them."

"Then maybe the real issue is that you're afraid to have him meet your family. The Devereaux clan can be a bit intimidating."

"I doubt that the Ayatollah could have intimidated Dillon. It's just that the timing is all wrong. The whole relationship is still too new. It may not even be anything important. Why subject it to all this outside scrutiny?"

"You don't believe for a single minute that it's unimportant," Beth said with feeling. Catherine stared at her in surprise.

"You sound so sure, far more confident than I do. How come?"

Beth rescued the filmy negligee from Catherine's nervous grasp and waved it in the air. "This. You're far too proper and cautious to be taking along something this provocative if you're not already head over heels in love with the guy."

Beth's observation made her heart thump erratically. "I'm intrigued. I'm hardly in love," she contradicted, ignoring the thumping.

"Intrigued doesn't call for silk and lace. Mad, passionate love calls for silk and lace. Are you trying to convince me you don't have the hots for Dillon?"

Catherine recalled the tender seduction of his lips, the provocative caresses. Heat flooded through her. "I'd say that's a pretty apt description," she admitted ruefully. She gazed at her neighbor beseechingly. "Beth, what am I going to do? I am not the sort of woman to have weekend flings. It goes against everything I was brought up to believe in."

"We're not talking casual sex here. You and Dillon are beginning to care for one another. And there's absolutely nothing wrong with a weekend fling," Beth said staunchly, "especially if it's the natural progression of a meaningful relationship."

Catherine regarded her skeptically. "What pop psychology book was that in?"

"No book. That's from a romantic bill of rights. It's about time you studied them. The next one is don't be late. Finish packing and get out of here. Have yourself a wonderful time. If Dillon can put those sparks in your eyes, then he has to have something pretty special going for him."

From the envious gleam in Beth's eyes, Catherine could tell exactly what her friend thought that something was. And while sex appeal was a very strong part of the attraction, Dillon's kindness and strength were equally important. She could feel herself blossoming under his interest. She'd never felt brighter or more enchanting. She'd never felt more like a woman.

If only their lives weren't so very different. If only they lived in the same place, so the relationship could evolve more naturally. As it was, all this chasing around the country to be together added an unrealistic edge of adventure to the relationship. How well would it hold up under the light of everyday living? Since there was absolutely no way to know that yet, she finally decided to give up making herself crazy over it.

"Thanks, Beth," she said, giving her a hug.

"For what? Just go and have the time of your life. Thinking about your madcap weekend will keep me occupied while I'm folding the stacks of laundry."

Catherine was halfway to the car, when she heard the phone ringing. She tried to justify ignoring it, but she didn't have it in her. She kept imagining a friend in desperate need of someone to talk to, her father being carted off to the hospital, her mother trying one last time to persuade her to come to North Carolina for the long holiday weekend. The last almost kept her right where she was, but the next thing she knew she was fumbling for her house key and running up the front steps.

"It's probably one of those computerized calls for a carpet service," she grumbled under her breath as she yanked up the receiver. "Yes, hello."

"Catherine?"

"Dillon? Is everything okay?"

"Maybe I should be asking you that. You sound breathless."

"I was almost in the car when I heard the phone ringing. My conscience wouldn't let me ignore it."

"For once I owe something to your conscience then."

Her spirits plummeted at his dire tone. "Something is wrong."

"Yes. I'm sorry. I can't get to South Carolina after all."

Catherine tried to swallow her disappointment. "A problem at work?"

"Yes. A client in Los Angeles is thinking of switching firms. The account executive has tried everything short of giving him the next ad campaign free. I tried to find a way around it, but I can't. I have to fly out there."

"Of course you do," she said automatically. "I'll miss seeing you, though. I was looking forward to those walks on the beach you promised."

"So was I," he said, in a voice so thick with emotion that Catherine went still. "We don't have to be apart, though. Come with me to Los Angeles instead. I have a friend who's loaning me his place at Malibu. We can still have those long walks on the beach."

To her amazement, she was actually tempted. Changing plans on a whim had never been one of her strengths. Maybe she'd inherited her rigidity from her mother. Whatever the case, her marriage had only solidified her desire for an orderly existence. For a doctor, Matthew had been amazingly adept at maintaining a schedule. Or perhaps it had only seemed that way because he'd blocked such a huge percentage of his time for work in the first place. Personal plans rarely had to be shifted if they weren't made.

"Do I sense reservations?" Dillon asked.

"Yes."

"Why? We were going to be together. The only thing changing is the location."

"How would I explain that I'm traipsing off to Los Angeles?" She ignored the fact that she hadn't even had the nerve to explain that she was traipsing off to Hilton Head.

"You're thirty-three years old. To whom do you owe an explanation?" he began impatiently, then obviously caught himself. Lightening his tone, he said, "Or is there a jealous lover you haven't mentioned?"

Surprised, Catherine noted the edge of anxiety beneath the banter. "No lovers, Dillon, just a family that is not used to my gallivanting off on my own at the drop of a hat."

"Sounds like a pitiful excuse to me," he said, determinedly maintaining his light tone. She could hear the strain of his effort in his voice. "Maybe it isn't L.A. you're really worried about."

"What's that supposed to mean?" she asked.

"Were you having second thoughts about seeing me again? You sounded fine when we talked the other day."

She couldn't bring herself to admit that he'd hit the nail on the head. She was scared witless at the prospect of a long, romantic weekend alone with him. Though a part of her longed to take Beth's advice and plunge ahead, another part kept shouting caution. "I just told you that I was already out at the car when you called," she responded far too defensively.

"You could have been going out for groceries."

"I was about to drive to Hilton Head. Maybe I still should," she declared stiffly, fully aware that she was trying to pick a fight, but unable to stop herself.

Dillon sighed heavily and backed away from the argument. "No. I'm sorry. I just don't understand why you're so reluctant to do this."

Catherine forced a laugh. "Frankly, neither do I. Habit, I suppose."

"Maybe it's time to break it," he suggested with more gentleness. "Catherine, I really want to spend this weekend with you and I think you want to be with me. Don't let old fears hold you back from taking a step into the future."

Basking in his warmth and his effort to understand, Catherine felt her anxieties begin to fade. Finally, her pulse racing expectantly, she whispered, "Maybe it is time."

Dillon pounced with the acute sensitivity of one who always recognizes subtle shifts in mood. He obviously knew exactly when to press an advantage. No wonder he was one of the top advertising executives in the country. "Then let's do it," he said briskly. "I'll call my travel agent and she'll have a ticket waiting for you at the airport. You can help me seduce this guy into keeping his advertising account right where it is."

"Dillon, I don't know anything about advertising."

"But you do know all about seduction," he teased. "You've had my head spinning ever since we met. Believe me, the techniques are essentially the same."

Despite herself, Catherine felt flattered. "Could be interesting. What do I do if this guy starts suggesting weekend meetings halfway across the country?" she queried innocently, enjoying Dillon's quick growl of displeasure.

"Turn him down," he snapped with what she suspected was only slightly feigned ferocity.

"Maybe he's the type who won't take no for an answer. I hear there are men like that."

She heard his deeply indrawn breath, then, "Wait by the phone. I'll have my travel agent call you about the arrangements, Catherine. We'll discuss this further when I see you."

"Yes, Dillon," she said meekly, but for the first time in years she wasn't feeling meek. She was filled with the satisfaction of knowing that she was able to turn the tables on a man, that her quick-witted responses could taunt and tempt. She felt, finally, like the Southern belle her mother'd been waiting all her life for Catherine to turn into.

The beach at sunset was a sight to behold—vibrant orange and the hottest pink splitting a sky of purest blue. There was no suggestion of the infamous smog to mute the colors.

"Beautiful, isn't it?" Dillon said, putting his arms around her from behind as she watched the waves wash over the wide stretch of beach.

"Glorious."

"Glad you came?"

She nodded.

"Me, too. I only wish we didn't have to go to this dinner. I'd much rather spend the evening out here with you, listening to the tide roll in and drinking champagne."

"Nice thought, but champagne makes me sneeze," she said. "The first time it happened, my parents were horrified. They wouldn't believe that a daughter of theirs had no tolerance for one of the finer things in life. They made my wedding hell because they insisted on serving champagne. I could have avoided it, I suppose, but everyone kept offering toasts and Matthew kept handing me a glass. By the end of the reception my nose was red and my eyes were watering." She giggled at the memory. "I figure it served him right that in all the pictures the bride looked as if she was just recovering from the flu."

"I'll bet you didn't laugh about it then," Dillon said.

She glanced up over her shoulder. "What makes you say that?"

"I'm sure you counted on everything being perfect to please your parents and your husband. Causing them even such a tiny embarrassment probably spoiled the whole day for you."

She turned in his arms and rested her hands on his shoulders. Her eyes were almost even with his. She felt as if he could see though to her soul. "You're amazing."

"I know," he said immodestly, his lips tilting in amusement.

"Stop it. I mean it. No one else saw how I felt."

"Probably because they were too worried about appearances and their own feelings."

"I'm painting an awful picture of my family, aren't I? They're really not like that. They just want what's best for me. The Devereaux have always maintained a certain life-style and my mother's family was doubly concerned with tradition. You can imagine what sort of monster a merger of the two families created."

Dillon shook his head and pressed his lips to her forehead. "No, sweetheart. That's not what I see at all. They created you, didn't they? For that I owe them my undying gratitude."

Catherine melted at the sweet sincerity of Dillon's words and the genuine appreciation in his eyes. "No one has ever said anything so beautiful to me before," she said, blinking back tears. One escaped and Dillon brushed it away with the tip of his finger.

"I will never grow tired of saying things like that to you," he promised. "I mean it, Catherine. You're just beginning to discover how much you have to offer. I hope when you fully realize your worth, you'll still want me in your life."

"I think I will always want you in my life," she said slowly, her heart suddenly filled to overflowing with tenderness and gratitude and something far deeper, an emotion so overwhelming she was awed by its intensity.

Dillon's mouth covered hers, capturing her breath, sharing his. In that passionate mingling a commitment was born, a commitment that she wasn't at all sure she was ready to make, but one that was un-

Catherine's smile remained fixed in place. "Mine wasn't."

"Never thought about that," Ruben said, turning to Dillon. "Why didn't you speak up, man? You know I don't pay attention to the social niceties. Too busy to pay attention. It's up to you to fix my image. Can't make any money producing those damned family films, if the public thinks I'm a low-class lout."

"You're absolutely right, Mr. Prunelli," Catherine said smoothly, before Dillon could even begin to gather his composure. He had to keep swallowing back his laughter.

"But you're obviously a very smart man," she said. "If you really put yourself into Dillon's hands, instead of just paying lip service to his advice, I'm sure he could turn around your image in no time. You might start by not referring to your movies as those *damned family films.* They're really quite good. I've taken my nieces and nephews to all of them."

Dillon finally found his voice. "She's right, Ruben. If you don't respect your product, why should anyone else?"

Prunelli appeared stunned by the barrage of criticism. Catherine was right, though. He was a smart man. Dillon could see the information being quickly absorbed. "Send me a plan," he barked. "By next Friday. If I like it, we'll keep you."

He pulled another cigar out of his pocket. Catherine's nose wrinkled in disgust and Prunelli chuckled. "Don't worry. I'm not going to light up 'til I get out of here."

She looked aghast. "But Mr. Prunelli, you've barely touched your meal. I hope you're not upset."

"Never finish," he said. "I'm taking three more meetings tonight. Can't eat four whole meals in one night. You two stay. Enjoy your dinner. It's on me."

He pumped Dillon's hand vigorously. "Keep her, Ryan. She's a breath of fresh air. Too damn many fakes out here."

When he was gone, Dillon turned his amused gaze on Catherine. She was looking miserable. Absolutely mortified. He'd never been prouder.

"I can't believe how rude I was," she said with a moan. "I just yanked that man's cigar out of his hand."

"He loved it. He's surrounded by sycophants. He meant what he said. Your honesty is refreshing. You kept the account for us. He knows the advertising was producing results, but the press was having a field day with him personally. You pointed out why."

"But I could have blown it. I didn't think. I just acted."

"Like a lady. Besides, it would have been worth it to see that look on his face. Now, let's stop talking about Ruben Prunelli and his smelly cigars. I have plans for the two of us for tonight...and tomorrow...and Sunday."

At the quick flaring of heat in Catherine's eyes, he felt a throbbing tension begin in his own abdomen. If he hadn't known it before, he did now: she was a woman who belonged by his side. Together they could accomplish anything. With her in his arms, he could reach heaven.

He held out his hand. "Shall we go?"

"No dessert for you, either?" she said, her voice suddenly tremulous.

"At home," he responded. "We'll share dessert at home."

Catherine's pulse raced as nervous anticipation sped through her. The drive to the beachfront cottage seemed interminable.

And far too short.

By the time they walked through the front door, she thought she'd die if Dillon didn't kiss her. Instead, he simply took her hand.

"Let's go for that walk on the beach. We've already delayed it far too long," he said.

The velvet night wrapped itself around them as they walked hand in hand along the cooling sand. Waves battered the shore, echoing the pounding of Catherine's heart. She shivered and Dillon stopped, pulling her into his arms

"Cold?"

The shudders abated and she sighed. "Not with you holding me like this."

"Then I won't let you go," he whispered huskily. Catherine lifted her gaze to meet his and what she saw in his eyes made her go weak with longing. Such obvious masculine appreciation. So much love.

"Catherine..." he began, then abandoned the thought. His lips molded themselves over hers— gentle, persuasive lips that robbed her of breath and filled her with joy. A fierce hunger began to build inside her, a need so primal, so intense that she swayed against him, seeking his warmth, aching for the feel of his bare skin next to hers. The desire was so all consuming, she was shaken by its force. Never had her body burned so. Never had she been so captivated by a touch.

Dillon's fingers traced the arch of her back, the curve of her hip. She moaned in response, alive as she'd never been before.

"Let's go inside," Dillon said.

"No," she whispered, her lips pressed to his neck. The skin was on fire, every bit as hot as her own. "Here, Dillon. Make love to me here. Now."

He opened his mouth to object, but she sealed off the argument with an urgent, demanding kiss that left them both trembling. Her fingers fumbled with the buttons of his shirt, then tugged it free of his pants. He groaned as she caressed the bare flesh of his chest. For one instant, she was startled by her own abandon, terrified by it, but then she was lost to the feelings, awash in sensation.

"You should have satin sheets and candlelight," Dillon murmured apologetically as he freed her breasts from the lacy bra.

"Starlight is better." In starlight, he wouldn't see her fear. Under the night sky, he wouldn't know the power of his touches. With the crash of the waves as background, perhaps he wouldn't hear the whimpers of pleasure that even now were building and building inside her. Matthew had never made her feel like this, never made her forget that she was a lady. In Dillon's arms she was discovering that she was a wanton, that there was a sensuality buried deep inside her that pulsed and burned and cried out for fulfillment. The hunger terrified her . . . and drew her inevitably.

Responding to her bold touches, Dillon stripped away the last of her clothes. For one awestruck moment, he stared at her and in his eyes she saw herself as a complete woman. She held out her arms and the last of Dillon's gentleness fled. His caresses became more intimate, his lips more possessive, his skin more beaded with sweat. His muscles quivered beneath her deep strokes until at last he sank to the sand, pulling her down on top of him.

She saw the flaring of passion in his dark-as-midnight eyes as he moved deep inside her. Once. Then again. Slowly and tantalizingly. Until there was nothing but the roar of the ocean and Dillon and the hot, urgent feelings that consumed and swelled and finally shattered inside her.

In that moment, Catherine knew she was lost. She knew that for however long it lasted, she would treasure what she had found with Dillon. It promised to be one hell of a ride.

# Four

_____

_Labor Day Weekend_

Catherine felt as though she were under siege. Dillon and her mother—two of the most unreasonable people she'd ever met—were coming at her from opposite directions. Her mother was emphatic about Catherine joining the whole family in North Carolina for the holiday weekend. Dillon was being just as pigheaded about finally getting away for that long-postponed weekend at Hilton Head. He sounded more tense and short-tempered than she'd ever heard him.

"What would you think about changing our plans for this weekend?" she asked cautiously.

"You can't be serious. I haven't seen you since July. As it is, I'm shuffling appointments right and left to make this work. I've made the reservations in Hilton Head and I have the plane ticket. I'm leaving New York in a few hours. Now's a hell of a time to talk about changing."

Catherine glanced anxiously toward the living room, then finally rolled her eyes. "You're right. I've been looking forward to it, too. Let's leave things the way we planned them."

There was a long pause before he finally said, "Are you sure? You aren't running scared on me, are you?"

She heard the concern, the quick shift to put her needs first. "No," she reassured him. "It's nothing like that. I'm as anxious to see you again as I ever was."

"Then we're all set. You have my flight number. Be sure to check on it so you don't end up waiting around at the airport in Savannah half the day."

"I'll check," she promised.

"Gotta run. I'll see you tonight, sweetheart. I can't wait."

"Bye, Dillon."

Catherine replaced the receiver and stood where she was for several minutes, before gathering the strength to face her mother again. She took a deep breath, then went back into the parlor where Lucinda Devereaux was just finishing her morning coffee.

"I'm sorry," she told her. "My plans can't be changed, after all."

Blue eyes sparkled with maternal indignation. "Now, dear, don't be stubborn. Nothing is that important. I'm sure you could make other arrangements for whatever it is that you have planned.''

''I don't want to make other arrangements, Mother. I'm looking forward to going to Hilton Head.'' That was quite possibly the most incredible understatement of her life. After being in Dillon's arms at last, she could hardly wait to have them around her again. The past few weeks without him had been incredibly empty. How could a city she'd lived in all her life suddenly be so lonely? Long-distance phone calls, no matter how frequent, didn't take the place of his touches or those darkly passionate looks that made her melt inside.

''What on earth is in Hilton Head, of all places?'' her mother demanded in a tone suggesting that, despite its long-running popularity with the rich, the resort was still far too new to be considered an appropriate destination. Moreover, Lucinda Devereaux was not used to being crossed, especially by her eldest daughter. Catherine had always been docile and accommodating. Obviously it was a habit she'd taken far too long to break.

''A man,'' she blurted before she could think of the consequences. ''I'm going there to meet a man.''

Shock registered on her mother's still lovely, aristocratic features. ''What man? Catherine, what on earth has come over you?''

''Nothing has *come over* me, Mother. I met someone. I've been seeing him for a while now. We're going to spend the holiday in Hilton Head and that's that.'' She was very proud of the firm tone of defiance, though she didn't hold out much hope that her mother would simply roll over and play dead.

"Do we know this man?"

"No. He's not from Atlanta."

As expected, her mother appeared scandalized by that news. "Then how did you meet him?"

"We met when I went to Savannah last year."

"Then he lives in Savannah," she said, looking relieved. "I know some lovely families in Savannah. Perhaps I know him, after all."

"No, Mother. He was just there on business. He lives in New York."

"Dear heavens!" Her mother sank back against the sofa and waved a handkerchief in front of her face. Catherine didn't buy the convenient attack of the vapors for a second. Sure enough, when she failed to respond, her mother sat up straighter and said with the force of a regal decree, "You must bring this man to North Carolina, then. That's all there is to it. I won't have you racing about to keep some sordid rendezvous with a stranger."

Catherine drew herself up with quiet dignity, proving that she was every inch her mother's daughter. "He is not a stranger to me and there is nothing sordid about it," she retorted. "No matter what you think, though, I absolutely refuse to spend what little time we have together parading him out for review."

Her mother's gaze was penetrating. A month ago or even a week ago, Catherine would have cringed under that look. Not now. Since knowing Dillon, she had grown stronger, more confident in her own decisions. "Are you ashamed of him?" her mother demanded. "Is he not suitable for a Devereaux?"

"His suitability is not the issue! He's a fine man."

"Then it must be us."

Catherine groaned. "Don't be ridiculous. I am not ashamed of anyone. If my relationship with Dillon appears to be turning into something permanent, then I assure you I will bring him home so that you can cross-examine him to your heart's content. Until then, I will handle this in my own way. Have a lovely holiday, Mother. Give everyone my love."

She dutifully kissed her mother's cheek, then spun around and left the room before her stunned mother could react. Catherine wasn't sure she could have withstood a full-fledged assault. Her mother was a master at instilling guilt and Catherine was still far too new at resisting. Only the prospect of having Dillon all to herself on a secluded beach had kept her strong. She wondered what it was going to take to brace her for the moment when she told her mother she was planning to start spending weekdays in Savannah going back to college...and seeing Dillon every chance he got to fly down.

She had finally gone through the Savannah College of Art and Design catalog after she'd gotten back from Los Angeles. In those first few days after her return, she'd felt as though she could conquer the world. A second college degree—this time in a subject of her own choosing—had seemed like a snap. She'd driven to Savannah on a Thursday, planning to meet Dillon for one night, only to discover on her arrival that he'd had to fly to Chicago instead. Though she'd been bitterly disappointed, she'd used the time to go by the school and enroll.

Then, as if to prove her commitment, she'd immediately searched for and found a small apartment in a carriage house. She'd been enchanted by the light that flooded in the high windows, the promising, but untended rooms and the old furniture that had been cast aside with such neglect. She had planned to tell Dillon about her decision when they'd talked later that night, but instead she'd held the secret as a surprise.

Catherine decided that she would tell him when they arrived in Hilton Head. Maybe they would even drive back into Savannah one day so he could see the apartment. Just in case, she dropped off a bottle of his favorite wine and stocked the refrigerator with food before going to pick him up.

At the airport in Savannah, she found herself pacing impatiently. The arrival board said his flight was on time, but she was so eager to be in his arms again, the minutes seemed to crawl by.

When he arrived at last, she was shocked by his appearance. He looked utterly exhausted. His rugged features were haggard, his eyes dull and lifeless until they came to rest on her. Then they brightened ever so slightly and his lips curved into a beguiling, tender smile.

"You are definitely a sight for sore eyes," he said, dropping his suitcase and pulling her into his arms. Catherine nestled against his chest and hugged him tightly.

"You, on the other hand, look like hell," she said bluntly, studying him with concern. "Bad week?"

"Lousy weeks," he said, emphasizing the plural.

She was astounded and admittedly a little hurt that he hadn't shared his problems with her. "But you didn't let on when we talked."

"The last thing I wanted to discuss on the phone was business," he murmured. "God, it feels good to hold you again."

Catherine was struck by a sudden brainstorm. It was late. Dillon was beat. Why should they drive all the way to Hilton Head when she had this wonderful apartment right here? "Let's get out of here and go someplace where you can hold me properly," she suggested.

"Improperly was more what I had in mind."

She grinned at him. "Me, too," she said with heartfelt enthusiasm.

In the car, Dillon's eyes drifted closed at once. Glancing over at him, she watched his struggle to keep them open. He stared out the window, then frowned.

"This isn't the way," he protested when she turned onto the highway into downtown Savannah.

"I know," she said, her eyes directed straight ahead.

The silence that greeted her response was so long, she finally glanced in his direction. He was wide-awake and regarding her curiously. "What do you have in mind, Catherine Devlin?"

"You'll see," she said, thoroughly enjoying the unexpected chance to be mysterious.

When she pulled up in front of a stately old house facing one of Savannah's many squares, Dillon's curiosity turned to obvious dismay. "Catherine, please. I'm too tired to go visiting."

"We're not going visiting."

"What is this, then? One of those bed-and-breakfast places? I hate that. There's not enough privacy."

"Have a little faith, mister. Grab your bag and follow me."

After a lengthy pause in which he seemed to be considering her rare display of bossy teasing, he gave a resigned shrug and took his suitcase out of the back seat. Catherine led the way through a yard filled with the heavy scent of roses in full bloom. A side path, lit by old-fashioned gas lamps, wound around to the back, where the old brick carriage house sat at the end of an overgrown cobbled drive.

"Who lives here?" Dillon asked, regarding the building with a critical eye.

"Do you like it?"

"It has a lot of charm. Whose is it?"

"Mine," she said, watching his eyes. They widened in surprise as they met hers.

"Ours," she said hesitantly. "That is, if you want it to be. I mean for whenever we can meet here. What do you think? Dillon, say something."

A slow smile began to play about his lips. "You bought this place?"

She shook her head. "I rented it. It was cheap. It's been fixed up some, but there's still work to be done.

They agreed to keep the rent down, if I'd do some of the restoration. The college sent me over.''

Suddenly his arms were around her again and he was swinging her in the air. "You enrolled!"

Laughing, she nodded. For the first time the decision seemed real. For the first time she allowed her excitement to show. Once she began telling him, the words spilled out. "I start classes this fall. I'll probably only stay here during the week. I'll need to get back to Atlanta on the weekends to make sure the house there is kept up and to do all the family things. I've cut back on my committees, but there were a few I was committed to helping. I can catch up on all that on weekends, too. What do you think?"

"I think you're wonderful. I am so proud of you."

The expression in his eyes wiped away the last traces of doubt. She lifted her hand and touched the tired lines on his face, lines that had almost, but not quite vanished in his enthusiasm for her decision. "Want to stay here with me this weekend?" she whispered. "There's food in the house. We wouldn't have that long drive. It would be like really living together, even if it is just for a few days. This will be the first place that will be ours together."

"You haven't stayed here?"

"Not yet. I was waiting for you. I wanted to share my first night here with you."

His eyes darkened with some emotion she couldn't identify. Pleasure. Passion. A vague hint of laughter. "You weren't planning to go to Hilton Head at all, were you?"

"Of course I was," she insisted indignantly, then wondered herself if that was the truth. "I just thought maybe we could stop here on the way back. I didn't get the idea for staying until I saw how exhausted you looked. What do you think?"

"I think we never will get that weekend in Hilton Head." He took her hand. "Let's go inside, so I can greet you properly."

She shook her head as she clasped his hand more tightly. "You promised me improper. I'm going to hold you to it."

Catherine was finally in her element. Dillon could tell as he watched her at work in the tiny kitchen. Wonderful aromas were emanating from the oven. She was humming under her breath. Though the apartment was furnished haphazardly, every piece of furniture in it gleamed. A bowl filled with roses sat in the middle of the tiny dining room table. Awed by her knack at creating a homey ambiance so quickly, he wondered briefly if he'd been wrong to push her to return to school. Still, she seemed happy about her decision. For the moment, he'd have to take her enthusiasm at face value.

He came up behind her and slid his arms around her waist.

"I'd rather have you than dinner," he said, nibbling on her ear. She smelled of lavender, a scent far more subtle than what she usually wore and twice as enchanting.

She squirmed against him in a half-hearted attempt to get away. The movement was maddeningly provocative.

"When was the last time you ate a proper dinner?"

"About as long ago as the last time I had you in my arms."

"Food first," she said staunchly, though he could tell from the shiver that ran through her that she was just as hungry as he was to experience that rare joy they had found together in Los Angeles.

When dinner was on the table, she watched every bite he put in his mouth. The close attention began to nag at him.

"More green beans?" she offered.

"No."

"How about more chicken?"

He shook his head. "If I eat any more chicken, I'll start clucking." He reached over and took her hand. "Sweetheart, you don't need to fuss over me. I'm all grown up."

Though his reproach had been mild, she looked as if he'd slapped her. Dillon felt like a heel. That quick flash of hurt in her eyes wiped away his impatience. "Catherine, I didn't mean that I don't appreciate what you've done. The dinner was wonderful."

"What's so wrong about my wanting to fix you a nice meal for a change?" she said stiffly.

"Nothing. I'm just not used to anyone worrying about me. And I'm definitely cranky. Everyone at work is ready to quit if I don't come back in a better mood. Don't you turn tail and run out on me, too."

She sighed and that awful look in her eyes began to fade away. "I'm not about to run out on you," she said finally. "But, Dillon, the last thing I want to do is smother you."

"You're not smothering me. I really am sorry if I sounded as if you were. Now come around here. I've eaten my vegetables and I'd very much like dessert."

"I baked an apple pie."

"It'll keep. I have something much healthier in mind."

Catherine came around to sit in his lap. Though her arms were around his shoulders, she was holding herself so rigidly that Dillon knew at once that she was still hurting from his unthinking criticism. He'd waited weeks for this moment, weeks longer than he'd anticipated and he ached from the loneliness of it. Though he'd worked harder than ever during their separation, for once his career hadn't blocked all other thoughts from his mind. Always there had been the memory of Catherine taunting him. Now he'd spoiled their reunion by taking his lousy mood out on her.

"Forgive me," he whispered in her ear. A sigh shuddered through her. She nodded finally and her arms tightened around him.

"Then show me," he pleaded. "I've missed you so much. I haven't been able to concentrate on any-thing. And at night, after we'd talk, I'd lie awake for hours wishing you were there with me, so I could touch you. Here." His fingers stroked the fullness of her lips. "And here." He circled the tip of her breast, thrilling as it responded to his touch. "You've missed me, too?"

"I thought I'd die from loneliness," she admitted, her fingers already at work on the buttons of his shirt. Her lips found the hard-throbbing pulse at the base of his neck, lingering, teasing his flesh with her tongue, then leaving it to cool it the sultry air.

Dillon's arousal was swift and urgent. His breath snagged as her hands began to stroke and caress his shoulders, then his back and finally his bared stomach. "Catherine, sweetheart," he began, then moaned with pleasure. "Catherine!"

"Hmm?"

"Do you suppose, just this once, we could actually get as far as the bedroom?"

"How utterly boring," she taunted, her blue eyes smoky with passion. "But if you insist...."

He lifted her into his arms. "I'm afraid I do. If we make love on the dining room floor, that is where I'm very likely to spend the night. Tomorrow I'll have aches and pains in muscles I'd forgotten existed."

"I'd be happy to massage them for you," she said generously.

"I'm tempted," he admitted, noting the wicked gleam in her eyes. "But all things considered, I'm opting for bed. I promise to try very hard to keep it from being boring for you...."

"Where did you learn that?" she asked a few minutes later, gasping for breath.

Dillon grinned. "Unless you've been married to a man for forty years, I'm not sure it's a good idea to ask him where he learned how to make love. Unless, of course, you're really angling to discover his past sexual history. Did you want references for this?'' he inquired as he stroked and teased in a way that left her writhing beneath him.

''No,'' she whispered raggedly. ''Just don't stop.''

''Not even for this?'' he taunted. ''Or this?''

Catherine gasped again, then arched into his touch. Whispering his name, her eyes wide with surprise, she trembled beneath him. His own body aching for release, he watched as hers slowly began to relax again.

A tear slid down her cheek as she touched his face. ''Why?'' she asked.

''A gift,'' he said. ''I wanted you to know how much I love you.''

A second tear clung to her dark lashes, then rolled down her cheek. ''Oh, Dillon,'' she whispered, her hands tangling in the hairs on his chest. ''I love you, too. You've already given me so much. You've given me back my self-confidence. I'll never forget that.''

She moved until her long, shapely leg was draped over his thigh and they were laying hip to hip. Her heat was as alluring as any flame and he found himself seeking it, reaching for the hottest center. There was little finesse to her movements, just an instinctive sharing, an overwhelming desire to enhance his excitement. She asked with anxious eyes and then she gave, urging him higher than he'd ever been before, crying out with him when they reached the top. It was a cry of exultation, of joy and of love.

When Catherine finally woke up in the morning, Dillon's place in bed was cold and empty. She glanced at the bedside clock. It was barely seven-thirty. For a moment, she panicked, wondering if he'd left, wondering if she hadn't been forgiven for last night's tension after all. Then she smelled the aroma of coffee brewing and heard the pop-up sound of the toaster. After several minutes, when there was still no sign of Dillon, she got up and pulled on her robe before padding barefooted into the kitchen.

She found Dillon seated at the kitchen table, papers spread all over, a cup of coffee and a plate of partially eaten toast beside him. He was wearing jeans, but no shirt or shoes. He looked impossibly sexy and every bit as tired as he had the previous night. She wanted to yell at him, to tell him he was killing himself, but had learned a bitter lesson the night before. He wouldn't appreciate it. She bit her tongue and simply dropped a kiss on his forehead as she passed by on her way to the coffeepot.

"Good morning," he murmured distractedly. "You're up early."

"I missed you. What time did you get up?"

"About six, I guess. My mind started turning over all this work I have to do, so I figured I might as well get started."

"I thought this was a holiday."

"It is. I'm not in the office."

"That's a lousy definition of a holiday," she said, struggling to keep her tone bantering. "Want some breakfast?"

"I had coffee and toast."

"No eggs? Bacon? Maybe French toast?"

"Nothing, really. I won't be able to relax until I get this done." His smile was apologetic, but his eyes were distracted.

Catherine nodded finally. "I'll leave you to it, then."

"Thanks," he murmured, but he was already absorbed again by what he was doing.

Catherine took a shower, then dressed in shorts and a T-shirt. She stood in the doorway of the kitchen and announced, "I'm going for a walk. Can I bring you anything?"

He glanced up, his gaze lingering appreciatively on her bare legs. "I wish I were going with you."

"Then come. It might relax you. You'll get even more done when you get back."

For an instant, he looked tempted, but then that familiar determined look came into his eyes and he shook his head. "Sorry, sweetheart. Not now. Maybe after dinner."

"Fine," she said, once again choking off her concern. How long could he continue with this sort of demanding pace? She had been able to delude herself on their past meetings that though Dillon was a self-avowed workaholic, he did permit himself some moments of release. Now she wondered. Had their previous meetings really been all that carefree? For the most part they'd been hurried. Only in Los Angeles had he seemed to relax once their meeting with Ruben Prunelli was over. Was her ability to distract him fading already or was it simply that Dillon was so compulsive about his work that no woman could ever compete for long? Certainly it had cost him his marriage. He'd already admitted that much.

Feeling every bit as lonely as she had during the weeks when Dillon had been in New York, Catherine walked until well past lunchtime. Only when she was practically starving did she return to the apartment. Dillon's papers were still strewn over the table, but he was on the sofa, a dictating machine in his hand, a thick report on his stomach. He was sound asleep, snoring softly, the tired lines in his face finally relaxed.

Catherine bent over him and smoothed his brow. "Oh, Dillon, how is this ever going to work? We're not even together when we're in the same room."

He sighed at the sound of her voice and stirred slightly, then settled more comfortably on the sofa. Catherine left him to sleep, while she ate her lunch. Then she began fixing dinner. She chose one of her favorite recipes, a complicated one which required endless chopping and mincing and stirring. It kept her hands busy, but unfortunately not her mind. The thoughts that tumbled about like colors in a kaleidoscope weren't nearly so pretty.

By the time Dillon awoke she knew that they were going to have to talk about the way he was working himself to death and, just as important, the way he was shutting her out. When he came into the kitchen, though, sleepy-eyed and contrite and loving, her doubts and criticisms slid away.

It became the pattern for the rest of the weekend: enchanting evenings, tumultuous lovemaking and then long empty hours of mental, if not physical, separation. It was their final morning together before she found the courage to confront him.

"Dillon, how do you feel about this weekend?"

He regarded her blankly. "It was wonderful. I loved being here with you."

"That's just it. You weren't with me. For all the time we really spent together, you might must as well have been in your office in New York."

"But I wasn't. I was here, even though it probably would have made more sense for me to stay up there. I came because I missed you, because I wanted to be with you. Why are you just bringing this up now? We've had the whole weekend and you haven't complained once. I thought you understood. Now, just when I'm ready to leave for the airport, you tell me that you've been miserable."

"I know. I should have said something sooner. I was trying to understand, but the truth of the matter is that I don't. Or maybe I do. Maybe you're more like Matthew than I thought. Maybe you like having a woman around for convenience, but don't want to make the effort necessary to keep the relationship alive."

His jaw tightened at the reference to Matthew. "I am not your ex-husband and I do not regard you as a convenience. I love you," he said angrily, yanking up the phone.

"What are you doing?"

"Calling a cab."

"I'll take you to the airport."

"I think not. I think it would be better if you stayed here and thought about what a real relationship is like."

"And you?" she countered furiously. "What are you going to be thinking about? Work?"

"Yes, dammit. I'm going to think about work. It gives me enough money to go where I want and to be with a woman I love, a woman I thought was starting to love me." He stomped through the front door, leaving Catherine to stare after him, openmouthed and trembling.

It was only after her fury had died down, after the loneliness had set in worse than ever, that she began to think about what he'd said. Never once all weekend had she asked him what he was working on. Never once had she wondered if there was some serious problem that demanded all of his energy. She'd been far too concerned with her own sense of loss, her own conviction that once again she was involved with a man with whom she'd come second.

It was going to be three or four endless hours before she could call Dillon in New York, an eternity before she could try to talk this out without anger and recriminations. She turned on the news which featured several holiday features. Labor Day. She lifted her glass of wine in a solemn toast to the occasion.

The phone rang as she was contemplating the irony. Her heart skipped a beat. Only Dillon had this number.

"Yes," she answered shakily.

"It's Dillon."

"Where are you?"

"Someplace over Virginia, I think. There's a phone on the plane. I called to say I'm sorry."

"No, I'm the one who's sorry. I shouldn't have added to your stress."

"And I shouldn't have shut you out. Want to try this again in a couple of weeks and see if we can get it right?"

Catherine felt a wave of relief sigh through her. The familiar pins-and-needles excitement began again. "Absolutely."

"I'm glad. I'll call you again when I get home."

"I'll be waiting."

Forever, she thought as she hung up. If that's what it took for them to make a life together, she would wait forever.

# Five

***

*Oktoberfest*

It was nearly midnight by the time Dillon finally called Catherine back. She was still sitting up in bed, half-asleep, trying not to worry and already beset by loneliness.

"Sorry to call so late," he murmured in the familiar low tone that sent her pulse racing. "Were you asleep?"

"Almost." She curled up and held the phone tighter, as if that would bring him closer. "What happened? There wasn't a problem with the plane, was there?"

"No, nothing like that. I stopped by the office. My assistant was there trying to resolve a crisis. Before I knew it the night was shot."

Catherine felt a chill creep through her at his words. So much for good intentions. She sat up just a little straighter. "Are you home now?"

"Yes. I just got here. I wish I were still there with you, though. I miss you already. I wish I'd had one last kiss to think about, instead of all those harsh words."

"Me, too," she said in a voice thick with regret. "Any idea when you can come back?"

"Actually, I did have one idea. I was reading an article in the in-flight magazine about Oktoberfest in Savannah. It's one of those first Saturday things they do down on the waterfront. We could drink beer and eat sausages and maybe dance a polka or two. How about it?"

She could tell he was trying to make amends, trying to prove to her that the next visit would be different, that they would have more time together. No matter how many doubts she had that he could change, she owed the relationship that chance. "Oktoberfest in Savannah, huh? It may not be Munich, but it sounds like fun. I'm up for it, if you are."

"I wish I could get back there sooner, but the way my calendar looks, it's not likely." His voice dropped seductively. "Will you keep my spot warm?"

"Absolutely," she said, rubbing her hand across the pillow that was still fragrant with the scent of him.

"Good night, sweetheart. I'll dream about you."

"I'll dream about you, too," she said softly. And count the days until Oktoberfest, she thought as she finally turned out the light and pulled his pillow into her arms.

As it turned out, the days flew by for once. Her classes began and were far more demanding and twice as exciting as she'd anticipated. She spent long hours after class talking with her fellow students and her professors. Dillon had been right. They did tend to look at her as a natural leader because of her experience. She basked in the mental stimulation. It was like being exposed to sunshine after a long, dreary winter. She had to force herself to go back to Atlanta on the weekends and face her mother's frowning disapproval. Her father made the trips bearable. Though he seemed somewhat bemused by her decision, he quietly gave her his support.

"You finish that program and we'll start looking around Atlanta for a worthwhile project," he said, ignoring his wife's scowl. "Maybe it's time I gave something back to this city by saving one of those fancy old buildings."

Pleased, Catherine threw her arms around him. "Dad, thank you for understanding."

"It's good to see you find your own purpose in life," he said, amazing her with his perceptiveness. "What about that young man your mother tells me you've been hiding from us? How does he feel about this?"

"He's the one who urged me to go back to school. I think he's really happy for me. We talk every day and he's coming down from New York next weekend."

Her mother looked up at that and her frown of displeasure grew. "We'll finally meet him, then?"

Catherine winced at having opened up an all-too-familiar can of worms. "Not really. He's coming to Savannah. We thought we'd go to Oktoberfest."

"Catherine!"

"What?" she said, her expression deliberately blank, though she knew exactly why her mother had reacted the way she had.

"That's so common."

"Mother, really," she said, unable to prevent a laugh. "It should be fun. Maybe you and Dad should drive down."

Her mother looked horrified, but there was a glint of amusement in her father's eyes as he said, "What about it, Lucinda? As I recall, there was a time when we could do a pretty mean polka."

Her mother flushed prettily. "If you think I'm going to swill beer and dance in the streets at my age, you have another think coming, Rawley Devereaux. Besides, we have theater tickets next weekend. We couldn't possibly go to Savannah."

Catherine sighed. "Maybe next time then. I really do want you to come down and see my apartment."

"It is hardly *your* apartment," her mother objected. "It belongs to some landlord. I really don't see why you insist on living like some transient."

"Would you rather I had bought a house in Savannah?"

"Of course not. You have a perfectly good house here in Atlanta."

"I can hardly commute from Atlanta to Savannah on a daily basis."

"You don't need to commute at all."

Catherine turned to her father and gave a helpless shrug.

"Don't mind her," her father said. "She hates having her chicks leave the nest."

Catherine regarded him and then her mother in astonishment. "But I left the nest when I married Matthew."

Her father grinned and patted her mother's hand consolingly. "Ah, but she thought you might come back after the divorce."

"I did not," her mother denied hotly, but the pink tint in her cheeks said otherwise. "I know perfectly well that Catherine is a grown woman now and has every right to make her own decisions. If she wants to live in somebody's garage, I suppose that's her business."

"I'll remind you of that, Mother."

To her amazement, there was a twinkle in her mother's eyes as she said mildly, "Yes, dear. I'm sure you will."

At the airport on Friday, Catherine studied Dillon's expression and determined that he looked decidedly guilty. She regarded his luggage suspiciously, then poked at his briefcase. "How much work is hidden in there?"

"Hardly anything," he vowed, though he didn't quite meet her gaze.

She gestured toward the carry-on suitcase. "And in there?"

"Nothing."

"Then why do I get the feeling that this weekend is going to be very much like the last one we spent here together?"

"Because, unfortunately, you are a very intuitive woman."

"Oh, Dillon."

"It's not so much the paperwork this time," he said, his attitude so determinedly cheerful that Catherine's fears mounted.

"What then?"

"Ruben."

Her stomach plummeted. "Pruneface?"

"Prunelli. He has a big public appearance coming up and he needs my assistance to prepare himself for it. He's getting an award for his contribution to the trend bringing back family pictures."

"Who on earth's giving it to him?"

"Catherine, he has made a contribution. There were three pictures in a row that no one else would take a chance on. Everyone thought the market for G-rated pictures was too soft. He turned them into box-office blockbusters."

"Okay, I won't try to take that away from him, but what about *Ninja Chaos* or whatever it is that came out last week? Now there is a really high-class piece of filmmaking. At least fourteen people had been killed or maimed before the opening credits finished rolling."

She almost laughed at the expression of horror that crossed Dillon's face. "What on earth do you know about that? You didn't see it, did you?"

"I can understand your astonishment. Actually, I did. Some of the kids from school were going. They invited me along."

Dillon started chuckling, which only made her more indignant. "I would have given almost anything to be there," he said. "How much of the movie did you actually see?"

"Not much," she admitted. "After the first ten minutes, I concentrated very hard on eating my popcorn one kernel at a time. I do not want the producer of that awful movie in my house."

"He won't be. He's taking us to dinner."

"Pruneface? Here? Why isn't he out in L.A., where they apparently think he's a genius and he can take four meetings in a night?"

"Because he needs my advice right now and because I insisted that the meeting would have to take place in Savannah or not at all. Remember when you're looking down your nose at him that you're the one who saved the contract for me."

"My mistake," she said with a moan. Then she regarded Dillon closely. "You actually told him he had to fly here if he wanted to meet with you, and he agreed?"

He nodded. "Actually, I think he's anxious to see you again."

"Heaven help me then. I will try to be polite, Dillon, but do not expect me to keep my mouth shut if the subject of that Ninja thing comes up."

"Just be yourself. Even though you're impossibly bossy, he seems to like you. I, however, have far more passionate leanings where you're concerned. Do you suppose we could go home?''

''Home?'' she repeated, suddenly smiling. To demonstrate her goodwill, she even picked up his briefcase, then linked her arm through his. ''I like the sound of that.''

''So do I, sweetheart. So do I.''


Catherine's goodwill almost lasted through the entire evening. Dillon knew the precise moment when she lost patience with Prunelli. He was amazed it had taken so long. She had tolerated the cigar, primarily because the producer had refrained from lighting it until after dinner. She had even ignored Prunelli's overindulgence in the wine and his enthusiastic consumption of beer when they'd taken a stroll along the busy waterfront. He had plunged into the spirit of Oktoberfest with gusto. Catherine had looked pained, but had kept silent.

Then the man who was being honored for his family pictures had spotted a trio of women half his age. He'd set out to woo them. When he pinched one and delivered a sloppy kiss to the cheek of a second, the last of Catherine's patience fled.

''Mr. Prunelli,'' she snapped, pointedly ignoring Dillon's eyes. ''For a man who is about to receive an award for the family values imparted by his films, you are behaving like a juvenile delinquent. If the press ever got wind that you'd been pawing and grabbing at women young enough to be your daughters they'd have a field day. Your production company would become a laughingstock, if that manipulative Ninja thing hasn't already made it one.''

Prunelli blinked several times as he tried to focus on the woman who was facing him, hands on hips, eyes flashing with indignation. ''Come on, Katydid,'' he said, his words slurring. ''Don't be mad. Just having a good time. Nothing else to do in this town.'' He peered around for Dillon. ''How do you stand it, Ryan? Never mind. You have Katydid. Hell of a woman, Katydid. Hell of a woman. Not scared of me. Like that. Too bad she's yours.''

Dillon leaned over and whispered, ''I told you he liked you.''

Catherine struggled against a smile, but lost. She supposed the man did have certain endearing qualities. ''Mr. Prunelli, maybe we should just take you back to your hotel, so you can get some sleep.''

''Sleep?'' he repeated, as though the word were alien. ''Never sleep more than a couple hours. Lighten up, Katydid. Let's have fun. Come dance with me.''

He took her hand and hauled her to her feet. Dillon started to intercede, but Catherine waved him back. ''It'll be okay. Maybe a brisk polka will wear him out.''

Instead, though, the dance seemed to revive him. It was two in the morning before they were finally able to drop him at his hotel room and go home themselves.

When they finally got back to the apartment, Catherine kicked off her shoes at the door and collapsed on the sofa. "Are all your business meetings this strenuous?"

"Strenuous? I'm fresh as a daisy."

She regarded him malevolently. "Sure. You weren't waltzing with the Hindenburg."

Dillon moved to stand behind her. His fingers began to work at the tight muscles in her shoulders, massaging until she moaned with pleasure, her head thrown back. The pale column of her neck, exposed and vulnerable, drew him. He leaned down and pressed his lips to the satiny flesh. That exotic floral scent she loved was every bit as alluring as a field of scented wildflowers. He wanted to bury his head between her breasts, to be surrounded by her heat, to be captured by her quick responsiveness.

He needed very much to love her. He had watched her tonight as he might a stranger. He had seen new facets in her personality that intrigued him. He had witnessed for the first time the strength she had attained since that night more than a year ago, when she had been lost and alone and vulnerable. He had a feeling that keeping pace with this new Catherine was going to require a man not easily intimidated, a man not threatened by a woman's dawning self-confidence. This was what he had wanted for her; this was the power he'd suspected was just waiting to be tapped. For a few brief moments, he'd been taken aback by it, but now he knew how right he'd been to encourage her to stretch and grow. Catherine Devlin was definitely becoming a woman to be reckoned with. If he didn't want her so badly as his wife, he might very well have offered her a job as his partner.

Anyone who could tame Ruben Prunelli with a glance could take on Manhattan.

"Dillon," she murmured sleepily. With her dark hair spilling loose and her lips pouty from his kiss, she looked more seductress than power broker. The fact that she was quickly becoming both took Dillon's breath away. He couldn't imagine what his life would have become if he hadn't met her.

"Yes, love."

She lifted her arms to him in a gesture that was at once innocent and powerfully provocative. "Take me to bed," she whispered.

With his blood pounding through his veins, Dillon scooped her up. "Gladly, sweetheart. Gladly."

Catherine slid out of bed while Dillon was still sleeping. She was delighted that he finally seemed to be getting some rest. After a quick shower and her usual half grapefruit, she settled herself on the couch to study for a Monday exam. She was still reading and making notes, when Dillon finally wandered out two hours later.

"What's all this?" he said, indicating the papers.

"Homework."

He grinned. "My lady the student. I like the glasses. I've never seen you wear them before."

She pulled them down and peered over the rim. "I just wear them for reading. You want some breakfast?"

"It's closer to lunchtime. Why don't we go up to one of the inns for lunch? Has Ruben called?"

"Nope. He's either sleeping in or he's found his one true love and is chasing her around one of the squares in town."

"If he's found his true love, Mrs. Prunelli is going to be slightly put out."

Catherine's head came up so quickly, her glasses almost slid off. "Some woman is actually married to that man?"

"Very happily, from what I understand."

"Since when? Last week? No one could take him longer than that."

"Twenty-five or thirty years. Actually, they're one of Hollywood's real marital success stories. Don't you ever look at all those supermarket tabloids?"

Catherine didn't deign to acknowledge that. She regarded Dillon suspiciously. "You're putting me on. Was she some Vegas showgirl or something?"

"High school sweetheart, actually."

"Dillon Ryan, I don't believe you. I don't believe that man went to high school."

"Your bias is showing." He actually seemed delighted about it.

"You bet it is. You're making it up."

"It is in the press releases. I put it there myself."

"That doesn't necessarily reassure me. I know all about Hollywood press releases. The accuracy bends like a willow."

His expression turning grim, Dillon advanced on her and bent down. He placed one hand on either side of her hips. "Are you accusing me of lying?"

She supposed he meant to sound menacing. Instead, he was terribly seductive. She wanted those clever lips of his to come another inch or two closer until she could taste them again. "I am," she murmured.

He levered himself between her thighs. "Then I guess you'll just have to be punished."

"Sounds intriguing."

His lips quivered, but he managed to hold back the laugh that clearly threatened. "You're becoming a terrible wanton, Mrs. Devlin."

She grinned and shoved aside her books. "I know. Isn't it wonderful?"

Then her arms were around him, his weight was satisfyingly heavy on top of her and his mouth found hers with unerring accuracy. The contact released an inferno and as the fire raged between them, she whispered raggedly, "Dillon, I need you so much."

"I know, sweetheart. I know." Clothes were stripped away or pushed aside until finally they were united again. "You have me," he promised. "Always."

*Always* only lasted an hour. They showered together, made love again, then Catherine finally sighed ruefully. "I really do have to study."

Dillon pulled her back into his arms. She buried her face against his still-hot flesh. Her tongue savored the salty taste of him, but this time the thought of all the work she had to complete before Monday wouldn't vanish in the haze of sweet sensations that had held them captive.

"I'm sorry, Dillon. I really do have to get back to work," she said.

"Couldn't you study after I leave tomorrow night?"

"There's too much to read. I'd be up the whole night. I may be anyway, even if I get through this one text today."

"Are you going to stay with it all day?"

"Just another hour or two. I promise."

His brows lifted. "I suppose if I objected you'd say something about turnabout being fair play."

"I would never hold up your own behavior as an excuse," she said with exaggerated piety. She grinned. "But if the shoe fits..."

"Go. Study. I can sneak in some time on my own paperwork now without feeling guilty."

"I suppose you can," she said. She went back to her place on the sofa and Dillon spread his papers over the dining room table. They took turns refilling the coffee cups. As she poured what she'd vowed would be one last cup, Dillon snagged her arm.

"See how companionable this can be."

She compared the long nights of studying alone to the past few hours. She supposed he did have a point. "We are together."

"Exactly."

"Maybe the problem last time was that I had no real interests of my own to pursue," she admitted.

"Maybe so."

She regarded him with an arch expression. "What happens when I get to be even busier than you?"

"Then I'll be the one grumbling about being abandoned." He smacked her on the bottom. "Until then we'll be content with what we have. Won't we?'' he said pointedly.

Catherine realized suddenly that she truly was content. She went back to Dillon and slid her arms around his neck from behind, resting her head atop his. ''We're very lucky, you know that?''

''I think I do.''

''Do you think it'll get better than this?''

She felt his shoulders grow stiff. ''Better how?'' he asked cautiously.

''I don't know. We can't spend the rest of our lives running back and forth between cities.''

''Right now that's the only choice we have,'' Dillon said.

''I know,'' she lamented.

She could tell from his tone of voice and his almost imperceptible withdrawal that it was not a topic to be pursued now. Though her remark had been made without thought, now that the seed had been planted she couldn't get it out of her mind. It sprouted and thrived like a deadly weed, choking off all the good thoughts. Contentment fled in the blink of an eye.

How long could they go on like this? It was unrealistic to expect that a commuter arrangement could work indefinitely.

*How long,* she wondered time and again. Those two words, hanging like a shadow over the future, threatened to take away every bit of pleasure she had felt in the wonderful present she and Dillon were sharing.

# Six

---

*Halloween*

"**W**here would you like to meet for Halloween?" Dillon asked in a low seductive murmur. Since he'd returned to New York this last time, the calls had grown more frequent than ever. He woke Catherine up each morning and was on the phone again to whisper good-night. Since his day often didn't end until midnight, it was wearing her out. Dillon seemed capable of surviving on four or five hours of sleep a night. She could not. She was turning into a walking zombie.

"I can hardly wait to see you in a costume," he said. "What would you choose, I wonder?"

"A witch," Catherine murmured sleepily. "Dillon, it's almost one o'clock. Can't we talk about this in the morning?"

"I love talking to you when you're all muddle-headed," he argued. "I get my best responses then."

"You mean I give in more easily then, which is exactly my point. I'm hanging up so I can get some sleep. If I don't, you're liable to talk me into wearing harem garb and going trick-or-treating."

"An interesting possibility. You'd be fascinating in all that billowing, see-through stuff. Now all we have to decide is where to go. Halloween is only a couple of weeks away."

She yawned and tried to think coherently. Halloween was not a national holiday. Apparently, though, Dillon was ready to use any excuse to see her again. At any other hour of the day that realization might have pleased her. "People do not get a day off for Halloween," she informed him. "Don't go getting some crazy idea about a long, wild-and-crazy-weekend. I have classes."

"Couldn't you play hooky for a day? People who've just won a potential six-figure account for a candy company practically swoon at the thought of Halloween, official holiday or not."

That jolted her up. "Six figures for candy corn?" she said incredulously.

"Well, not candy corn," he admitted. "Something slightly more upscale."

"You must live in a ritzier neighborhood than I do. Not even my parents give out Belgian chocolates to trick-or-treaters."

"Maybe not this year, but by the time I finish with this ad campaign, they will next year."

That piqued her curiosity. "You're representing some Belgian chocolate manufacturer?"

"Not exactly. Actually, I took on that candy company on the waterfront in Savannah. It'll give me a third reason to come down there more regularly."

"Third reason?"

"White Stone, you and now the candy company."

"I'm glad I rank higher than nuts and chocolates. Is this the place where we spent a fortune the last time you were here?"

"Where you spent a fortune," he corrected with ungentlemanly accuracy. "Yes, that's the one."

"Dillon, I thought you said this account was going to be profitable. That's a tiny little operation."

"With huge mail-order potential."

At first she'd thought his decision entirely capricious, but she was beginning to see the sense of it. The candy was delicious. "So that's what you were talking to the owner about while I was overdosing on pralines."

"That's right. Even chocophobics won't be able to resist, once I get finished with touting the virtues of their pecan fudge and pralines."

"And that gives you satisfaction?"

"That gives me the time and money to meet you someplace over Halloween and, yes, it brings me tremendous satisfaction to watch some small local company go big-time because of my work."

"Remember that the next time you want to spend an entire weekend wooing a jerk like Ruben Pruneface. He doesn't need you."

"That's not what you were saying when you ripped apart his image. As big as he is, he definitely needs a make-over. I think this firm can do it for him."

"At heart, though, he'll still be an arrogant, egotistical boor."

"A *rich* egotistical boor. And I thought you liked him. Once you robbed him of his cigar in L.A. and discovered he could polka, you seemed to get along famously."

"I wouldn't go that far. But you're missing my point."

"Which is?"

"If you applied the same high standards to your clients that you do to your ads, you would not deal with the Ruben Prunellis of the world."

When Dillon stayed silent for several seconds, Catherine wondered if she'd gone too far. Just because she hadn't liked the studio executive didn't mean Dillon shouldn't work with the man. She had no place meddling in his business decisions. Handling Prunelli's studio probably did bring Dillon a certain amount of prestige, despite the man's personal obnoxiousness.

"Maybe you're right," he said finally, cutting off the apology she was ready to offer. "I never thought of it that way. You are judged by the company you keep. I tell my clients that all the time. Maybe it's time I started practicing what I preach. Of course, Prunelli did take me on to change his image, along with selling his movies. Doesn't that show that his heart's in the right place?''

"Or his pocketbook. Let's drop it. When you get right down to it, I had no right..."

"Of course, you have a right to your opinion. That's one of the things I love about you. You're honest to a fault once you finally get the courage to open your mouth. Poor Prunelli didn't know what hit him, when you told him you thought his last block-buster success was a manipulative piece of trash.''

Catherine groaned. "I might have hated that Ninja garbage, but I could have been a little more diplomatic for your sake.''

"Absolutely not. Even I enjoyed watching the way his eyes bulged and his mouth kept opening and closing like a fish. I doubt he'd ever been rendered speechless before. Unfortunately, in no time he probably forgot all about it.''

"Certainly by the time he'd finished the second bottle of wine.''

"Tell me the truth. You enjoyed telling him what you thought, didn't you?''

She thought it over. To be honest, it had felt good. "I have to admit, I did. Does that make me a terrible person? I actually liked seeing that sleazy man squirm.''

"That just makes you human, sweetheart. You spent too many years reining in your opinions. I'm glad you're learning that the walls won't collapse if you say what's on your mind.''

"The walls may not collapse, but I could cost you millions.''

"In my business, knowing when to be blunt is an art. I think you're a natural at knowing the best timing. Prunelli asks about you every time we talk. You've definitely made a lasting impression."

"He's probably trying to make sure I'm not in the vicinity," she said, unable to control another yawn. "Dillon, I have to get some sleep. People are beginning to ask about the circles under my eyes. They seem to think I'm suddenly leading a life of nonstop debauchery."

"If only that were true," he said with a heartfelt sigh. "Go to sleep, my beauty. We'll settle this Halloween thing in the morning."

True to his word, Dillon was back on the phone before 7:00 a.m. He sounded wide-awake and disgustingly cheerful.

"I've made a decision," he announced.

"Good for you," she grumbled, wondering just how guilty she'd feel if she skipped her nine o'clock class and slept until noon.

"Don't you want to hear it?"

"Tell me," she said. Maybe then he'd go away and let her dream about the nicer, gentler Dillon who only kept her awake to do wonderful, exciting things to her body.

"I'll fly in on Friday and then first thing Saturday we'll drive over to Hilton Head for the weekend. The weather's still nice. Most of the tourists have probably headed home. We should have the whole beach practically to ourselves. We can sleep late Sunday morning, have breakfast in bed."

*Sleep late? Breakfast in bed?* Now the man was talking her language. "Make the reservations," she said, then hung up and pulled the pillow back over her head.

The trip to the beach turned out to be just what they needed. They arrived by midday on Saturday, checked into their hotel, then for lunch, found a place with a view of the water. They lingered for hours over the seafood and wine, talking and catching up on all the little details of their lives that they never seemed to find time to discuss in their hurried phone conversations.

With sweaters wrapped around their shoulders and their pant legs rolled up, they walked the beach hand in hand until the sun finally began to fade and the pine- and salt-scented air grew uncomfortably chilly.

As they walked back to the hotel, Dillon slowed and turned her to face him. Catherine reached up and smoothed the lines of his face. "You look more relaxed than I've ever seen you."

"And you look even more beautiful."

A sigh of pure pleasure caught in her throat. There was something almost bittersweet about the rare quiet moment. Deep inside, where her heart called the shots, she had this weepy, desperate feeling that they were reaching a terrible turning point, a make-or-break time in their lives.

Over the past couple of weeks whenever she'd allowed herself, she'd thought about where the two of them were headed with their lives. No matter how romantically she viewed their love, she couldn't avoid the reality. What they had wasn't the stuff of happily-ever-after. Oh, she loved Dillon and deep in her heart she believed that he loved her, but what they were building together was a make-believe existence.

That night, as she slept in his arms, she felt as though it was all slipping away and there was nothing she could do to change it. Tears clung to her lashes, then spilled onto his chest. He stirred restlessly, but fell into an even deeper sleep when she brushed his face soothingly with her fingertips. She traced his wide brow, his nose, the tiny scar at the corner of his mouth. When she stopped to think about what she was doing, she realized she was trying to memorize Dillon, to learn the scent and texture and shape of him for the empty nights she feared were ahead.

In the bright, clear light of morning, she tried to tell herself to stay silent, to hold on to what they had for however long it lasted. Their love was special. There was no reason to ask for more, but then she realized that was exactly the problem. As good as it was, she did want so much more.

At breakfast she toyed with her food. Dillon watched her closely, but apparently her odd mood had communicated itself to him because he was far more subdued than usual. There were no teasing remarks, no provocative looks.

"It's warm outside," he said finally. "Why don't we take a blanket and spend a couple of hours on the beach? Maybe the fresh air will make you feel better."

"I feel fine."

"Then why so glum?"

She stared at him helplessly. "I don't know if I can explain it."

He held out his hand. "Let's go outside. We'll talk when you're ready." His patience in the face of her inability to communicate her worry made her feel like weeping.

A few minutes later, they had changed their clothes. Dillon's gaze traveled over her appreciatively. "I like the duds. Or maybe I should say the lack of them. That's a helluva bathing suit for a former debutante."

She'd thought the bright blue suit was a modest one-piece until she'd seen the look of masculine approval in Dillon's eyes. Maybe the neckline did reveal a little more than she'd realized of her full breasts. Maybe the high French-cut styling showed off a little too much leg. She reached for a long T-shirt, but Dillon touched her hand.

"I like it," he reassured her. "Any woman would kill to have a figure like yours. And every man on the beach is going to envy me."

She blinked back unexpected tears. "How do you always know the right thing to say?"

Dillon appeared startled by her intensity and by the sudden tears. He reached for her and held her close. "Sweetheart, what's wrong?"

Once again, she took the coward's way out and merely shook her head. "Let's go outside."

When they found a secluded cove, Dillon spread out the blanket, then stretched out beside her. Her gaze drank in the sight of his well-muscled legs, the flat stomach and broad shoulders. Without a word, he handed her the suntan lotion. She applied it with fingers that trembled. As if each touch might be her last, she caressed and lingered until she could tell by the look in his eyes and the set of his jaw that he was losing the struggle not to respond.

"Your turn," he said finally, his words hoarse.

His hands were gentle as he massaged in the cool lotion. She gave herself up to the pure sensual delight as he stroked her back. He followed the line of her suit as it dipped to just above the swell of her buttocks. Then he coated each leg, slowly, provocatively, lingering at the erogenous spot behind her knee, the sensitive curve of her calf. He even applied the lotion to her feet, his hands sure and confident as they followed the curve of each instep and tenderly stroked each toe. Her whole body was aflame by the time he was done, the heat spreading from a point low in her abdomen until even her cheeks felt flushed.

Forcing herself to turn over and sit up, she caught the expression on Dillon's face. It was a painful mixture of desire and hurt, of longing and confusion. Troubled brown eyes met hers and in a voice that barely held steady, he asked, "Catherine, what's wrong? Have you met someone else?"

She reached out and took his hand, holding it tight against her cheek. "No. No, nothing like that. I swear it."

A sigh shuddered through him. "Then tell me, please. I think I could take anything but that."

She drew in a deep breath, tried to find the right words, then said simply, "I think we're getting to a turning point and I'm afraid."

His eyes filled with puzzlement. "What sort of turning point?"

"This isn't enough for me anymore. I don't want to live from month to month, waiting for the weekends you can get away, praying that some business crisis won't interfere with our plans." Avoiding his gaze, she lamented, "What we're doing isn't real."

Waiting for him to reply, she dug her toes into the warm sand with sensual appreciation. She could feel Dillon's eyes on her. He reached out and trailed a finger the length of her thigh. The touch raised goose bumps.

"Deny the reality of that," he challenged in a low voice that sent yet another shiver of pure delight running through her.

"Oh, Dillon, that's very real. I can't deny all the physical attraction. You've brought me alive again. I feel things with you that I'd never imagined possible. It's the one thing that's never been a problem with us."

"Then nothing else matters."

"Of course it does. We can't spend our lives running away from home for these idyllic interludes. We're romanticizing the relationship. We live in a constant state of anticipation. We're so anxious not to spoil what little time we have that we ignore the petty little frustrations. We avoid dealing with anything that isn't pleasant until it's almost too late."

"Then marry me. Will that be real enough for you? Will that give you enough time to talk about the frustrations?"

She closed her eyes against the anger that was building in his expression. "I'm not challenging you to a duel, Dillon. I'm not looking for drastic solutions. I just want us to face what's happening realistically."

"Meaning what? What do you really want, Catherine? Do you want to move to New York and live with me and see how it goes? Do you want to set a schedule, to take turns commuting weekends? Your place one weekend, mine the next?"

"At least that would make more sense than what we're doing now. Do you realize you've never met my family or friends, that I've never seen your apartment or met your children?"

"You may not know the color of my wallpaper or the size of my bed, but you know everything that's important about me."

"Do I really? I don't think the picture can possibly be complete without knowing the little details of day-to-day living, without getting to see how you interact with your kids, with the people who work for you. They're an integral part of who you are, Dillon."

"Then come to New York. Come for Thanksgiving. Stay for a week, longer if you can. You can send me out the door to work in the morning and have dinner on the table at night. You can see whether or not my closets are neat. You can check out my office and listen to my kids grumble about whatever you fix for dinner. Will that be real enough for you?''

"It would be a start,'' she said solemnly, ignoring the sarcastic tone that had crept into his voice.

He shrugged, feigning a display of disinterest. ''Then let's do it.''

"Don't make it sound like the beginning of the end, Dillon. If we're not heading toward a life together, then maybe we're wasting our time.''

"Is marriage the only kind of relationship you want to have with a man? Is it impossible for an Atlanta debutante to simply fall in love, to take one day at a time?''

Catherine couldn't think of how to answer that. There had been a time only a few short months ago when she'd been convinced that she never wanted to be married again, when one day at a time might have been enough. Knowing Dillon had changed that. She'd begun yearning again. Not just for a husband, but for a family, for the closeness that two people have when they live together, when they commit to happily ever after.

"A piece of paper doesn't guarantee happiness, Catherine,'' he said as if he'd read her mind. ''You and I both know that.''

"No. But if we're not willing to work at what we have now, how in the hell will we ever dare to consider more?''

"Will you be satisfied with less?'' he asked in a hushed tone.

She felt as if the sun had gone behind a cloud. She shivered in the suddenly icy atmosphere. "Is that all you're offering?" she asked slowly.

He uttered a harsh curse, then ran his fingers through his hair. "I don't know what I'm offering. Until a few minutes ago, I could have sworn that all I wanted was to spend the rest of my life with you, married or not. As soon as the subject of the future came up, though, I felt like a fighter pilot who's trained all his life for a mission and suddenly discovers he's terrified to fly into combat. I guess I have more battle scars than I'd realized."

Catherine laughed despite herself, though there was a certain bittersweet edge to the humor. "I'm not sure I'm crazy about the analogy, but I know what you mean. What's happening between us scares me, too, but I don't want to let my fears stand in the way of what we might have."

"Brave words," he said, his gaze intent.

She dared then to touch his cheek. "I don't feel very brave," she admitted softly.

He captured her hand and held it tight, kissing her fingers. "Neither do I, but if you're ready to move forward, then so am I. Thanksgiving week, okay?"

Catherine didn't think she could squeeze even a simple yes past the raw emotion that clogged her throat, so she nodded. Tears stung her eyes as they had earlier, but when the first one began to roll down her cheek, Dillon was there again to wipe it away. Patient. Enduring. Tender.

She had insisted on this daring, risky new course. Now she could only pray that he would always be there, because for the hundredth time that day alone she acknowledged how very much she loved him and how much she feared that she was wrong to want so much more than what they had right then.

# Seven

---

*Thanksgiving*

"What do you mean you won't be home for Thanksgiving?" Catherine's mother demanded, setting her silver teapot down with a thud that rattled the ancestral English bone china. "We have the entire family coming for dinner. Whatever will I tell them?"

"Tell them the truth, Mother. Tell them I'm in New York with Dillon."

"That man," Mrs. Devereaux huffed. "I don't know why you can't find some nice man right here in Atlanta. George Banes, for instance. He's always been partial to you."

"George Banes is sixty-five years old."

"He's rich and quite respectable."

"He's Southern. Isn't that what you really care about?"

"I do not have such a parochial view of the world, young lady. I just don't want you running off to live in New York. You're the only daughter I have left here in Atlanta now that your sisters have married and moved away."

It was the closest her mother had ever come to admitting out loud that she loved her. Catherine clung to the words, but she couldn't let them sway her. She leaned down and kissed the still-smooth ivory cheek. "I'm not going to run away anywhere. I'm just going for a long holiday weekend."

"And what about Christmas? Will you abandon your own family then, too?"

"We haven't talked about Christmas. We're trying to take this relationship one day at a time right now. This trip to New York is a big step for us. We've both made mistakes in the past by jumping into a relationship too quickly."

"Will you be staying with his family?"

"No. They live in Queens. We'll be in Manhattan."

"Catherine!"

"Mother, don't look so shocked. You know perfectly well what sort of relationship Dillon and I have."

"That doesn't mean I want the whole world to know it. In all these years haven't I taught you anything about maintaining appearances? Couldn't you stay at the Plaza or perhaps the Waldorf? It would look so much better."

"To whom? You and Dad already know where I'll be. Who else will care? You're just looking for anything to make me feel guilty and stay here."

Her mother sighed and lapsed into her thickest drawl. She'd perfected the role of martyr years ago, but she also knew when to quit. Not, however, without one final sniper shot. "I suppose I might's well save my breath. No one ever pays a bit of attention to me anyway."

Catherine had to fight to keep from smiling at her mother's resigned air. "You and Dad could come to New York, too, you know. Think how much fun we could have shopping. We could go to the parade. It would be wonderful."

"I have no desire to go someplace where I'm likely to be mugged."

"You're just as likely to be mugged here in Atlanta. I know perfectly well you've seen the statistics. You read every inch of type in the newspaper just to make sure that none of your social set has run amuck."

"Okay, I'm just too set in my ways to go running off over a big holiday. I'm getting old. I like having the whole family around me."

"If you start talking about your declining years, I'm going to get up and walk out. Don't try playing on my sympathies. You have more energy than I do. I will be here for Christmas, though. I promise."

She appeared partially pacified. "That man, too?"

"I'm sure Dillon will do his best to be here, too."

Her mother nodded, her expression suspiciously satisfied. "Well, then, I suppose that will just have to do." She picked up the teapot. "More tea, dear?"

Catherine noted that suddenly too-innocent expression with suspicion. She had the oddest feeling she'd just been maneuvered. "Nope," she said emphatically, before she could find herself unexpectedly agreeing to move back home, where her old room still had ruffled pink curtains on the windows and an extravagant doll collection on the bookshelves amid the leather-bound children's classics. "I have to run. I'll call from New York on Thanksgiving Day so I can say hello to everyone."

Her mother squeezed her hand tightly as Catherine leaned down to kiss her. "Have a wonderful time, dear," she said with unexpected gentleness. "It's about time you had some fun out of life."

Catherine stared at her in amazement. Even more improbably, her mother actually winked. "Why, you old devil," Catherine said.

"Remember that," her mother chided. "I'm not half as stuffy as you and your sisters think I am."

Catherine was still shaking her head in astonishment as she left to fly to New York the following afternoon. That momentary relaxing of her mother's reserve gave her a whole new perspective. She had a feeling when she got back from the holiday she ought to begin spending a bit more time with her mother to discover exactly what sort of a woman she really was. Maybe she'd spent too many years thinking of her only as a restrictive mother and not nearly enough time recognizing that there were far more facets to her personality.

When her plane landed at La Guardia, Catherine called Dillon's office. Helene Mason, with whom she was on increasingly friendly terms because of the number of phone calls she and Dillon made to each other, began apologizing the moment she heard Catherine's voice.

"I know he was supposed to be at the airport, Mrs. Devlin, but he was called into a meeting downtown. He called from the car phone not five minutes ago to say that the traffic is impossible because of the rain and everyone's trying to get out of town for the weekend. He'll never get there. He wants you to take a cab and meet him at his apartment."

Catherine felt her high spirits begin to sag ever-so-slightly. It was a small thing, but she'd really wanted Dillon to meet her at the airport. She sighed. "If you talk to him again, tell him I'm on my way."

"You shouldn't have any problem coming in. You should be at his place in twenty minutes or so. He'll wait for you downstairs with an umbrella. This rain is coming down in buckets. They say it'll turn to sleet or snow by tonight."

Terrific, Catherine thought with a groan. "Thanks, Helene. I hope I get to meet you before I go back."

Catherine made a valiant attempt to recapture her enthusiasm in the midst of the airport chaos. The baggage area was filled with tired, irritable travelers and tons of luggage that all seemed to look exactly alike as it circled past on the conveyor. By the time she found her two pieces and lugged them to the taxi line, she was exhausted.

The trip into Manhattan across the 59th Street Bridge went as quickly as Helene had predicted, but in town the traffic came to a rush-hour halt. "So this is gridlock," she muttered, sinking back against the seat as horns blared impatiently. At least it gave her some sense of appreciation for Dillon's inability to get to the airport.

He was, however, waiting at the curb for her. Dressed in a topcoat, his hair windblown and wet, his complexion ruddy from the cold, he didn't seem like the man she'd come to know over the last few months at all. There was a new tension about him, a vibrancy that excited her, even as it made her unaccountably afraid.

He reached over and practically lifted her from the car. "You're here at last," he murmured, pulling her close and kissing her. "Sorry about the airport, but it couldn't be helped. You've seen the traffic. It's a bear. Let's get inside before you get soaked." He hurried her through the lobby and into a glass-lined elevator, which rose quickly and smoothly the twenty-two floors to his apartment.

Inside, when their coats were hung to drip in the guest bathroom, she said, "I didn't know you had a meeting this afternoon."

"I didn't know about it when I called you this morning. It came up at the last minute. It's a big Wall Street account and when they want to talk, I have to go listen. Come on, let's get your things unpacked and then I want to take you out to dinner. We've been invited to join the Farrells for a drink at six. I've told you about them, haven't I? He's my top creative man. I've been thinking lately about making him a full partner. Maybe you can help me decide if that's the right way to go."

Catherine was so taken aback by the busy schedule Dillon had planned for their first night that his request for her decision-making assistance barely registered. She glanced at her watch and protested, "Dillon, it's already five-thirty. I need to change."

"No, you don't. You look beautiful. They're going to love you. And I can't wait for you to meet the O'Haras. They want us to stop by for a nightcap. Tomorrow we're having Thanksgiving dinner at the Plaza with the Petersons. It's an annual bash."

"A bash?" she repeated weakly. "How big?"

"I think they had fifty or so last year, mostly clients."

"But I thought we'd be having Thanksgiving dinner with your family."

"I told them we'd try to get by at some point over the weekend. We'll fit it in somehow. The Petersons are an important account for me."

"What about your kids? Maybe we could just get a turkey and invite them."

"They're going to spend the day with Paula's family. Then they'll come into the city Sunday. I told them we'd go skating at Rockefeller Plaza."

*"Ice skating?"*

"Sure. You skate, don't you?"

"No."

"We'll fix that. I'll have you skimming over the ice like an Olympic champion in no time."

"On my feet or on my bottom?"

"On your feet, I promise."

Catherine felt another attack of trepidation. She'd known what sort of life Dillon led in New York. She knew he was a high-powered executive. In fact, she had known from the beginning that was what had broken up his marriage. She was just beginning to understand why. There was a dynamic, full-speed-ahead side to his personality that matched the frenzied pace of New York. In Savannah it had been muted. She'd fallen in love with the charm and energy, but she wasn't quite prepared for the full force of Dillon in high gear.

As she went into the bathroom to freshen her makeup at least before they left for the evening, Dillon followed her, perching on the side of an extraordinarily lavish tub big enough for two. That tub aroused some intriguing ideas, but Dillon appeared oblivious to its proximity or its promise. He continued to run through his plans for the holiday.

"Dillon, if we cram all that in, when will we breathe?" *When will we make love?* She left that question at least unspoken. Maybe he didn't want her as much anymore. Maybe in this environment, he'd already recognized that she was out of place.

He dismissed her plaintive question with a wave of his hand. "I just want to make sure you have a good time. I talk about you so much that everyone wants to meet you. And that's what this weekend is all about, isn't it? You wanted to see how I live."

Catherine supposed she should feel flattered that he was so anxious to open his life to her. Instead, she felt overwhelmed. He was right. This was what she'd wanted. She didn't dare attempt to throw a damper on his enthusiasm. "Let the games begin," she muttered mostly to herself.

"What?"

She plastered on her very best smile, the one she'd used to effect at a hundred charity balls and boring dinners with Matthew's medical associates. "Nothing," she said, linking her arm through his. "Let's go. I can't wait to meet your friends."

She hated them. She had been with Evan and Shirley Farrell for precisely fifteen minutes and already her nerves were screaming for release. There was nothing really wrong with them. They were polite. They were delighted to meet her. They adored Dillon. But Evan laughed too loudly, drank too much and had the personality of a bulldozer in overdrive. Shirley, by comparison, was a timid gray mouse, totally overshadowed by her exuberant husband.

"Shirley, do you have children?" Catherine asked, hoping to find some topic that would animate the woman's dull demeanor.

"Two, a boy and a girl."

"How nice. How old are they?" she asked, genuinely interested.

"Seven and eleven. Evan thought that four years was the best spacing. They're friends, without being quite such rivals."

Catherine cringed inwardly. "I see. Are they involved in a lot of school activities? I know my friends seem to spend half their lives carpooling their kids. My neighbor Beth says she hasn't had control of her life since the kids were old enough to talk."

"Actually, I don't have to worry about that. They're in boarding school. They came home for Thanksgiving, of course, but they'll be going back on Sunday."

*Then, why are you here,* Catherine wanted to demand. Instead, she merely said, "You must miss them, or do you have a career that keeps you busy?"

"No. The house is large, though, and Evan likes to entertain. That takes all my time. We've tried several housekeepers and none of them can seem to get the work done to his satisfaction."

Catherine thought at once about how many times she'd made similar statements to Matthew's friends, always feeling a little ashamed that she wasn't doing more with her life. She felt sorry for Shirley and wondered if she'd been the object of similar pity for all those years she'd been content to bask in her husband's shadow.

Before she could try to instill some sense of renewed purpose in Shirley, Dillon was on his feet, explaining that they had dinner reservations. Five minutes later they were back in his car.

"Thanks for keeping Shirley occupied," he said. "You're terrific. I knew you'd get along with her."

"She's pathetic."

Clearly offended, Dillon turned to stare at her. "What's that supposed to mean?"

"She has no life of her own, no personality. She is exactly the way I was up until the divorce. I feel terrible for her."

"Don't. She's happy."

"Do you honestly believe that or have you never really talked to her?"

Dillon stopped for a red light and studied her curiously. "You're really upset about this, aren't you?"

She realized that he was genuinely worried. "I'm sorry. She just got to me because she sounded so much like I once did. It brought back a bad time in my life. I don't want to begin falling into that old pattern again."

"And you thought that's what was happening tonight?"

"It felt uncomfortably familiar. The men sitting around talking business, while the womenfolk chatted about inconsequential things."

"That's just part of business entertaining."

"I suppose so. Right now, though, it seems more like a dangerous trap."

The whirlwind of activity never slowed long enough for Catherine to take stock of it again. By Sunday morning she was exhausted and more frightened than ever. While she'd been increasingly aware that she was falling into a trap she'd sworn to avoid, Dillon had been in his glory. Every bit of entertaining had a purpose. There was not a single dinner or a single party that was held for the sheer pleasure of being with close friends. They had almost no time alone, except for the hours they spent in bed. Even their lovemaking seemed to adapt to the New York pace—more hurried and less satisfying.

Reluctantly she got out of bed, pulled on her robe and went into the dining room, where she knew she'd find him already engrossed in the morning paper, even though it was not yet seven o'clock. He looked up and smiled.

"I thought maybe you'd sleep late. I'm afraid I've worn you out."

"We need to talk," she said determinedly, sitting down opposite him and pouring herself a cup of coffee from the pot that always seemed to be at hand.

"You look so serious."

"That's the way I'm feeling. Dillon, don't you ever slow down?"

"Sure I do. I've taken this whole weekend off to be with you."

"Really? How many deals have you finalized since Friday night?"

He seemed bemused by the question. "Two, maybe three. I don't know. Why?"

"Isn't that work?"

"I suppose. What are you getting at?"

"That you haven't done one single thing just for fun since I've been here."

"Have you been bored? Is that it?"

"No, I haven't been bored. Not exactly. I just expected that this weekend would be different."

"How?"

"For one thing, I thought I'd get to meet your family."

"The kids will be here about nine."

"And your parents?"

He seemed uncomfortable. "I guess that's not going to work out this trip after all, but you'll be back. There will be plenty of opportunities for you to meet them."

Catherine sighed and gave up. He just didn't get it. Maybe he never would, even after losing Paula and the kids. He was happy filling his hours with nonstop work. Though he'd invited Catherine to be a part of that, he would probably have been just as content if she hadn't been there. Was there really any place in his life for the sort of relationship she'd dreamed of them having?

She was feeling more depressed than she had in those first weeks after her divorce, when the front door burst open and two miniature versions of Dillon came racing in. The two boys skidded to a stop at the sight of her.

"Hello there," she said, holding out her hand to the taller of the two. "I'm Catherine. You must be Jonathan."

He took her hand and pumped it energetically. "Yes, ma'am. This here is Kevin. He's only four. His hands are probably dirty, so you may not want to shake with him."

Catherine grinned. "Oh, I don't think a little dirt is going to hurt me." She took Kevin's grimy hand very solemnly. "I'm glad to meet you, too."

Jonathan giggled at that. Tossing his coat on the floor, he went tearing straight toward the den, where Dillon was on the phone with Evan Farrell about a deal that had nearly been lost the previous day. "Hey,

Dad, did you get the doughnuts like you promised? I want the jelly kind.''

Laughing, Catherine followed the children into the den. She could hardly wait to see Dillon's response to all this unbridled exuberance. Kevin was already scrambling onto his father's knee, while Jonathan waited impatiently for him to hang up the phone.

"Evan, I have to go," Dillon said, hugging Kevin to him. "I've been invaded by small Martians demanding food. Yes, I know doughnuts are not good for them. That's why they're a special treat." He glanced up at Catherine when he said it, his expression as guilty as if he'd admitted to income tax evasion.

When he'd hung up the phone, she teased, "Don't look at me. I'm not going to reveal your awful secret. Assuming, of course, that I get my share."

"Yeah! Come on, Dad. We're starving."

"I'm sure," Dillon said dryly. "How long has it been since breakfast?"

"Hours and hours. Besides, all we had was yucky oatmeal."

"Yucky," Kevin confirmed.

"I agree, guys. But it is good for you. Promise to keep eating it or no doughnuts."

The two boys exchanged serious glances, then nodded. "We promise."

"Good. Now who wants jelly and who wants cream-filled?"

Apparently this was a familiar game, because Dillon had just the right number of each. To her amazement, he even insisted on orange juice and milk to go with them.

"Hey, Catherine," Jonathan said, obviously accepting her presence without questions. "You gonna go skating with us?"

"I'm going to try," she said, her delight in Dillon's boys overriding for now her concerns about the future. The expression on his face as he watched them was almost painful to see. There was a yearning there she would never have suspected. Maybe he did realize how much he'd sacrificed, after all.

"She's never skated before, guys," he said. "We're going to have to teach her."

"It'll be okay," Jonathan reassured her. "Girls can learn how pretty easy. Mom did, huh, Dad?" His expression sobered slightly. "She doesn't like to come into the city anymore, though."

"But you do?" Catherine asked.

"You bet. We do neat stuff when we come to see Dad. He takes us to museums and movies and we even went to a play once. I liked it, but Kevin fell asleep."

"Did not."

"You did, too, you little dweeb."

Dillon scowled at him. "What did I tell you about calling your brother names?"

"Sorry, Dad. Can we go now? They have this really neat place right next to the ice rink. Dad always gets us hot chocolate there."

"One thing for certain," Catherine teased, her amused gaze meeting Dillon's. "These children will never starve to death."

"They're bottomless pits," he confirmed. "Now you see why I have to work so hard. I have to keep them supplied with doughnuts and hot chocolate."

"And pizza," Jonathan said.

"Hot dogs," Kevin countered. "We had pizza before."

"Guys, you've just finished breakfast. How about we take this one meal at a time? Now go bundle up."

They obediently scooted out of the kitchen, but not before dumping their dishes into the sink.

"They're good kids," Catherine said as Dillon stared after them. "I really like them."

He turned back to her and smiled. "They're what keeps me going. I was a little worried right after the divorce. Kevin cried a lot and Jonathan was angry, but I think they're finally adjusting. I think they're going to be okay."

"Because they can tell you still love them."

He pulled her into his arms and kissed her quickly. "Thank you for saying that. Sometimes I worry that I'm bungling things."

"Not that I can tell."

"Hey, Dad, aren't you two ever gonna get ready?" Jonathan demanded.

"They were kissing," Kevin observed, bringing a blush to Catherine's cheeks.

"Can't put anything past you two," Dillon said easily, taking her hand. "Let's go, everybody. I can't wait to get this lady on the ice."

After the first half hour, Catherine decided that only a masochist would ever go ice-skating. Her ankles bent in unnatural directions. Her bottom was sore and cold. Dillon patiently picked her up again and again. Even the boys tried to help by offering suggestions.

"Let us show her," Jonathan finally said, clasping one hand. "Kevin, you get on her other side."

He tugged her gently forward. Kevin hung on tightly with his tiny, mitten-covered hand. Taking smaller steps, she began to get her balance. Finally she tried to glide. She made it halfway around the rink before she realized that they'd let her go. She caught sight of Dillon. "I'm skating," she shouted. He lifted his hands and applauded. Jonathan's face was split by a broad, dimpled smile. She was almost back to them before her feet shot out from under her again. This time Dillon caught her before she hit the ice. She fell against his chest.

"Enough," she said breathlessly. "I demand hot chocolate and warmth. You all can stay out here and freeze to death, if you want to, but I'm taking a break."

"Me, too," Jonathan said loyally.

"I don't want to spoil your fun. You three can stay out here. I'll watch from inside."

"We'll all go in," Dillon decided. "Then we'll take another few turns around the rink before we go to lunch."

After hot chocolate, more skating and a pizza with everything on it, even the two pint-size bundles of energy admitted exhaustion.

"By the time we get back home, it'll be time for your mom to come by and get you anyway," Dillon said.

"Maybe we could stay over tonight," Jonathan said hopefully.

"I'm afraid not. You guys have school tomorrow and I have work."

"Mom says that's all you ever do."

Dillon watched Catherine as he admitted, "She may be right, Jonathan."

When they'd left amid hugs and promises from Catherine to come back again, Dillon led her into the living room, turned on the stereo and poured them each a glass of wine. She was stretched out on the sofa, when he came and sat beside her, pulling her across his lap. "Tired?"

She nodded. "But it's a nice tired. You're like a different person when you're with them, Dillon. The way you were today, that's the Dillon I first met in Savannah. That's the man I fell in love with."

When she looked up, his eyes were closed. His fingers idly smoothed her hair. He opened his eyes finally and met her gaze. "I want to be that man all the time, sweetheart. I really do. I'm just not sure it's possible."

She sat up and took his face in her hands. "Anything is possible Dillon. All you have to do is want it enough."

When her lips met his, the kiss began as a gentle reassurance. Dillon turned it into a tender promise. There was so much desire, so much longing in that kiss that it shattered her fears and left her filled with hope again.

# Eight

———

*Christmas*

It was barely eight o'clock on Christmas Eve, Dillon had been at her parents' house for less than an hour, her sisters and their families had yet to arrive and Catherine was already a nervous wreck. At this rate by the end of the holiday weekend, they'd have to commit her to one of those discreet sanitariums for a lengthy rest cure.

Wincing as her mother launched yet another enthusiastic anecdote about Matthew, Catherine took a deep breath and interrupted. "Mother, I'm sure Dillon isn't interested in how skillfully my ex-husband carved the turkey. He's a surgeon, for heaven sakes. What did you expect?"

"Catherine, don't speak to your mother in that tone," her father said, then resumed puffing on his pipe. His mild words didn't fool her. His quiet commands were always deadly serious. She cast a pleading look in his direction, then sighed in resignation and sat back.

"I was just trying to make a point," her mother said. "More canapés, Mr. Ryan?"

"Thank you. What point was that, Mrs. Devereaux?" Dillon said with apparent interest. Catherine felt like smacking him for encouraging the recitation. This was not going at all the way she'd hoped. She'd wanted Dillon to experience what a real family holiday was all about. Instead, he seemed to be undergoing one of her mother's finest trials by fire.

"That Matthew will be missed on holidays," her mother concluded with a triumphant gleam in her eyes. She was observing Dillon's reaction and missed Catherine's moan entirely.

"Not by me," Catherine muttered under her breath, then said aloud, "Dillon, wouldn't you like to take a walk? I'll show you the garden." She couldn't keep an edge of desperation out of her voice. Her mother ignored it.

"You'll catch your death of cold out there," her mother objected.

"Let them go, Lucinda. Can't you tell they'd like their privacy?" her father said indulgently.

"But the rest of the girls will be here any minute now."

"We aren't going clear to Macon, Mother. When everyone else arrives, have Maisie call us." She grabbed Dillon's hand and tugged him from the room.

"I wish I thought you were as anxious to be alone with me as your father thought," he said when they were shivering outdoors.

"I am." She circled his waist with her arms and rested her head on his chest. She felt better at once. "Why does coming here reduce me to adolescence all over again? I was a lousy teenager. I'm no better at it now. Thank you for agreeing to put up with this. I couldn't think of any way around spending Christmas here without causing World War III."

"You survived the tortures of New York with me. It's the least I can do. Besides, it gives me a chance to see how you managed to turn out to be such a sexy, dynamic woman," he murmured, brushing his lips across hers.

"Oh, I wish... I'm afraid you won't see much evidence of those qualities around here, if all I do for the next forty-eight hours is apologize."

"Then stop apologizing," he said, gently stroking her cheek with the back of his fingers. "Your mother's behavior is not your responsibility. Are you afraid I'm going to be put off because your mother keeps dragging Matthew out as an example of the highest masculine virtues?"

Catherine rolled her eyes. "What man wants to hear that his predecessor was the Rolls-Royce of husbands?"

He tilted her chin up. When she dared to meet his gaze, she caught the sparks of laughter. "Do you believe that Matthew Devlin was exemplary?" he asked.

"Hardly."

"Then it doesn't really matter what your mother thinks. Let her have her illusions."

"Believe me, she had no illusions where Matthew is concerned. She was just as rotten to him as she's being to you," she admitted ruefully. "You seem to be taking it better than he did, though. Matthew wanted very badly to impress her. He thought it would help him up the Atlanta social ladder. She saw straight through him. You probably impressed her by not running for your life."

His arms tightened around her. "Catherine, do you suppose we could stop talking about Matthew and your mother?"

"What did you have in mind?"

"I thought maybe we could do something to generate a little heat. It's cold out here."

"Good thinking."

"No thinking, Catherine. Just feel." With his mouth slanted across hers, with his hips hard and decidedly masculine against hers, and his hands splayed over her buttocks, it was all too easy to comply. The temperature rose by several degrees in no time at all. The prospect of facing her mother again seemed far less important than the solid strength of the man holding her tightly to him. And the memory of the very real problems they'd had in New York seemed very far behind. Maybe the magic of Christmas would make everything all right, after all.

The gleaming cherry wood table stretched a good eight feet down the length of a dining room that was larger than many New York apartments Dillon had visited. A centerpiece of pine and berry-laden holly added a festive note of color to the stark white damask placemats and napkins. Heavy crystal goblets and wineglasses sparkled in the candlelight from a huge old-fashioned chandelier. Unless he missed his guess, the gold-edged china and ornate sterling were family heirlooms, probably from some ancestor who'd crossed on the *Mayflower*.

Old money and staid ideas. Mrs. Devereaux had let him know practically in her first breath that she was a member of the Daughters of the American Revolution and proud of it. Catherine had already warned him that she was also staunchly Southern and had little tolerance for "damn Yankees." Not counting her insistence on bringing up Matthew Devlin every ten seconds, she'd been polite to Dillon despite his Northern roots. He had no illusions. It wasn't that he'd charmed her. Catherine and a sense of duty probably demanded she treat him reasonably well, at least in front of the rest of the family.

Besides he and Catherine, there were fourteen other adults seated around the table; the children had been banished to an equally lavish spread in the parlor. As far as he could tell, the grown-ups had little in common besides family ties, and it seemed to him that most of them weren't any more fond of each other than a sense of obligation required. All things considered, it was the oddest Christmas gathering Dillon had ever been part of, a Gothic ritual with undercurrents of hostility that fit every stereotypical idea he'd held of the starched Devereaux clan. It was so far from his own humble beginnings, he had absolutely no basis for comparison. His parents hadn't even been able to put a turkey on the table most years, but they'd managed to create a holiday atmosphere of warmth and laughter.

Here, only the free-flowing French wine kept the occasion from being deadly dull. In fact, as tongues began to loosen, Dillon anticipated fireworks. He was just getting interested in the ebb and flow of the tense conversation around him, when the elderly, blue-haired belle beside him put a gnarled, but perfectly manicured hand on his and drawled in a sweetly seductive tone that belied her age, "Why, Mr. Ryan, where ever has Catherine been keeping you?"

"In a closet," he whispered confidentially and enjoyed the confusion that flickered for only an instant in the depths of her quick, intelligent eyes.

"A closet?" she repeated skeptically, amusement playing about her pursed lips.

"Why, certainly. Isn't that where all the best-kept secrets are hidden?"

After another slight hesitation, she reproached him lightly, "Oh, Mr. Ryan, you are teasing me, aren't you?"

Dillon grinned and decided he liked this slightly dotty, aging coquette. "Yes, ma'am. I believe I am."

Her laughter was pure as a bell. "You young devil. I'm so glad Catherine found you. You're not at all like that stuffy ex-husband of hers."

"Matthew was stuffy?" According to Mrs. Devereaux's earlier recitation, Matthew had been the next best thing to a saint. Though he understood why she'd

trotted out the memory of her ex-son-in-law, he was
anxious for another view from a more impartial ob-
server.

"Dull as dishwater," she confirmed. "But don't
you dare say I told you so. Catherine's a very private
woman. She wouldn't like me spreading gossip about
her marriage. Still and all, a woman like Catherine
should have a family, don't you think so?"

"A family?"

"Children, Mr. Ryan, a whole houseful of them.
You look as though you could do the job," she said
bluntly. "You do want children, don't you?"

He'd never really given the question any serious
thought. He already had Jonathan and Kevin. He
found himself glancing across the table at Catherine
and trying to imagine a tiny version of that dark
beauty. The image took his breath away. "Yes," he
said softly. "I think you're right, Mrs. Brandon."

She nodded in apparent satisfaction. "You call me
Aunt Mildred, young man. I suspect it won't be long
before you're family, if you have any say about it."

"Not long at all," he confirmed impulsively before the older man on his left claimed his attention
with a brusque opinion on the disgraceful state of
banking.

"You're just as well off hiding your money under
the mattress as putting it into one of those savings and
loan places," George Franklin declared, waving a
shaky finger at Dillon. Like Aunt Mildred, he seemed
to be well into his seventies, but also like her, age
hadn't dimmed his wit one little bit. He leaned closer

and peered into Dillon's eyes. "Well, what do you have to say about that?"

"I think it's a matter of choosing the investment program that's best for you," Dillon said diplomatically.

"Bah! That's a wishy-washy answer, young man. What do you really think?"

"I think you're trying to get me into trouble, sir. I know perfectly well that you are president of one of the largest savings and loan institutions in the state of Georgia."

The old man threw back his head and hooted at the reply. "Done your homework, boy. I like that." He banged his fork against his water goblet to get the attention of the rest of the people at the table. "I'd like to propose a toast," he declared. "To Catherine and Dillon. May your love prosper along with your bank account."

At the foot of the table Mrs. Devereaux looked as if she'd been forced to swallow vinegar. A deep blush colored Catherine's cheeks as Dillon's gaze caught hers. Her sophisticated, cool veneer slipped away and she became once more the vulnerable, sensual woman with whom he'd fallen in love on that sultry, long ago night in Savannah. He grinned with unabashed enjoyment at the transition.

"Later," she mouthed, attempting to look stern.

"Indeed," Dillon replied, lifting his glass in a more private toast.

He had not counted on Mrs. Devereaux when he'd uttered that seductive taunt at the dinner table. Either the old lady was a mind reader or she'd long ago decided to do everything in her power to keep Catherine and Dillon apart. She sent the men off to the living room for cigars and brandy. The suggestion, which carried the weight of a matriarchal order, clearly startled several of the younger women, who were already on their feet.

"Sit down, Catherine, Melanie. We'll have our tea in here."

"But, Mother," Catherine protested mildly, only to be silenced by a look that would have withered the heartiest weed in the vast Devereaux gardens.

Grinning at Mrs. Devereaux's obvious ploy and Catherine's apparent frustration, Dillon bent over to whisper in her ear as he passed. "Try to bear up, darlin'. We menfolk will come to rescue you soon."

"Go to blazes," she whispered back just as sweetly as Mrs. Devereaux looked on disapprovingly.

Not bothering to hide his amusement, he winked boldly. "That's the spirit, sweetheart." It reassured him that she no longer seemed one bit intimidated by her mother's repressive actions. Only when he was casting one last lingering look back did he notice the glint of mischief in Lucinda Devereaux's eyes.

"I can't imagine what got into Mother," Catherine said later, when she and Dillon had finally managed to escape to the sun porch that swept across the southern side of the huge old house. Christmas lights twinkled in the yards of distant neighboring houses. If it hadn't been for her mother's attitude, it would have been a magical evening. She'd liked watching Dillon hold his own with Aunt Mildred and Uncle

George. This was the way she'd imagined things would be in New York. Instead, they'd spent all their time with business associates. Despite the quirky nature of her family, she loved them. She just didn't understand them all the time. "Why do you suppose she insisted on such an old-fashioned tradition? She never has before."

"She's protecting her chick from Northern invaders," Dillon suggested.

"I suppose that could be it," Catherine agreed.

"You aren't planning to let her intimidate you, are you?"

Catherine met his fierce gaze with a look that was pure southern belle. She wondered if he had any idea how manipulative her mother was capable of being, of the influence her mother tried to wield, not just over her, but the entire family. "I'm not the one she's trying to intimidate."

"You're wrong, my beauty. She read my intentions the first time she looked into my eyes. She's been preparing her battle plan ever since."

"Don't worry. It's been a long time since Mother has successfully run my life."

"But not so long since she's tried."

"It's in her blood," Catherine confirmed with an easy laugh that bore surprisingly little resentment. Over the past months she actually had come to terms with that. Maybe she was getting stronger and more independent after all.

"She would have made a wonderful queen, don't you think?" she said thoughtfully. "She loves waving her hand and watching everyone scatter to do her bidding. If she'd had her way, my father would have arranged marriages for all of us while we sat demurely in the garden and awaited word of our fate.''

''If that had happened, would you have gone along with it?''

Catherine thought it over, realizing that in many ways that was exactly how she'd come to choose Matthew—through the subtle prodding and encouragement of her parents. Her mother might not have been crazy about him, but she had found him suitable. ''I think perhaps I did,'' she admitted.

''And now?''

''Now I'll make my own choices.''

''Are you going to choose me, Catherine? Even if I don't fit in with your mother's idea of a respectable husband?''

''Who wants respectable?'' she taunted, refusing to be led into a serious conversation on the subject of marriage. Though the thought entered her mind with increasing regularity, she had yet to think of a way to make it work. At her age, she was just beginning to realize marriage often took more than love. Dillon's obsession with work was not something to be so easily overcome. And tonight was not a night for discussing anything that serious.

''I'm after your body,'' she said in an attempt to distract him.

She felt Dillon stiffen. His fingers caught her chin and tilted her head up until she was forced to meet his gaze. His eyes condemned the flip remark. ''Why would you say something like that? It sounds like a line from some silly romantic comedy.''

She kissed his cheek. "I was teasing, Dillon. You're always telling me to lighten up."

"Not when the subject is as serious as marriage."

"We were not talking about marriage."

"Weren't we?"

"Dillon, we've been over this and over this. We can't even think about marriage until we can figure out how to keep this relationship afloat. Your life is in New York. I can't imagine myself even visiting there more than a couple of times a year, much less living there."

"So much for whither thou goest."

"Exactly. Unless I miss my guess you feel exactly the same way about Atlanta."

"I have nothing at all against Atlanta, but my business is in New York."

"And my life is here or will be as soon as I finish school in Savannah. That's another reason why I can't very well pack my bags and go traipsing off to New York. You pushed until I enrolled. I'm happier than I've ever been. Do you expect me to walk away before I graduate?"

Dillon sighed. "No," he admitted with obvious reluctance. "I'm glad you're taking the classes. You're obviously more focused now, more self-confident. But what happens when you do graduate? Will you be willing to work in New York then?"

"That's too far down the line even to contemplate."

"So you want us to put our life on hold until then?"

"Isn't there room for compromise?"

"Offer me one," he said reasonably.

But as hard as she tried, Catherine couldn't think of a solution that was any more workable than what Dillon was asking. Finally, though, she was forced to admit that they'd simply been dancing around the real issue, at least as she saw it. "Dillon, it's more than simply choosing a city to live in. I don't like the way you are in New York, the way we are," she finally said wearily. "We were at each other's throats the first night. We had no time alone. You barely take the time to be with your children. You plan your entire life around business functions with people you barely know and don't even seem to like very much."

"That's the nature of the work I do. Are you saying you want me to give that up?"

"Of course not. But couldn't you modify it just a bit, separate your work and your personal life a little more?"

He refused to meet her gaze as he paced around the room. "I don't know. I honestly don't know. But I do know that I love you. That I want this to work more than I've ever wanted anything. Come back with me now, Catherine. Let's try it again until classes start after the first of the year. If we can talk about what's not working, we can handle this. Please, sweetheart. Give it another chance. The kids are dying to see you again. New York is especially beautiful this time of year. We can spend New Year's Eve in Times Square."

The very idea made her shudder. "Not in this lifetime," she vowed fervently.

He grinned at that. "Okay, a quiet dinner just for the two of us at the fanciest restaurant in the city. We can dance 'til dawn. No business." He touched his lips lightly to hers, sparking a fire deep inside her. "Please," he urged, his tongue caressing the curve of her mouth. A delicious shiver raced through her. There was no place on earth she would rather start the new year than in Dillon's embrace. If she was going to have to brave the gray gloom and idiotically fast pace of New York to be in his arms, then brave it she would.

This time.

"When do we go?" she asked as he pulled her willingly against him.

"We could sneak out tonight, but I'm trying to win points with your mother. I suspect that's not the way to do it."

"Good guess."

"Then we'll leave in the morning after dutifully paying homage to the queen and opening our gifts."

"Don't let her hear you call her that. She doesn't know that's how my sisters and I think of her."

"Coming from me, though, she'll just think it's her due," he said dryly.

"Oh, Dillon," Catherine said as a low chuckle escaped. "I do love you so."

"I love you, too. And we're going to make this work. I promise you that."

# Nine

---

*New Year's Eve*

For a while Dillon thought it was going to be all right. When they first got back in the city, they played tourist. They saw a play, an off-Broadway production that Catherine loved and he hated. They argued about it for hours over cappuccino and cannoli in a Little Italy bakery. They went to an exhibit at the Museum of Modern Art that she found offensive and he found fascinating. Without wasting her breath, she dragged him into a taxi, asked to be taken to the Metropolitan and tugged him into one of the galleries, waving at the paintings by the Old Masters.

"That's art," she told him.

"But if artists only painted portraits and landscapes in that style, they'd stagnate. Art is a creative medium. It's supposed to change and evolve. That's what you said about that play that didn't make any sense."

Cheeks pink and eyes flashing, she stared back at him. "Well..."

"Come on, Catherine. Admit it. I'm right. Experimentation is important."

"I never said it wasn't," she said huffily.

"Didn't you?"

"No. I just said I didn't like *that* experimentation. Now take me to lunch. All this debating is making me hungry."

"Where would you like to go? The Russian Tea Room, maybe?"

She shook her head. "That deli in your neighborhood. I have a craving for pickles."

Dillon stopped in his tracks, bemusement settling on his face. "A craving for pickles?"

Catherine nodded. "What's so odd about that?"

*"A craving for pickles?"*

She regarded him blankly, then finally her eyes widened in understanding. "Oh, for heaven sakes, Dillon. I'm not pregnant."

"Are you sure?" he said, his throat clogged with sudden emotion. He remembered the way he'd felt on Christmas Eve when Aunt Mildred had suggested that Catherine ought to have a houseful of babies. "It would be okay. In fact, it would be wonderful."

"Dillon, it would not be wonderful. Call me traditional, but I do believe couples ought to be married before they become parents."

"No problem. We could be married by tonight. I can't think of a better way to spend New Year's Eve."

There was an odd expression on her face, just the tiniest hint of longing, but she was quick to tell him, "Silence those bells, Romeo. The only aisle you and I are walking down in the immediate future is in Bloomingdale's. I want that dress I saw in their holiday catalog."

"We'll just see about that," Dillon vowed.

"The dress?" she inquired.

"The wedding."

"Don't try to turn this into a contest of wills, Dillon. The only way you'll ever change my mind is by showing me that we can make it work."

"And how am I supposed to do that?"

"Time."

"We've known each other for nearly two years."

"Yes, but we've only actually been together about a month if you add up all our visits."

"Be sure to tally in the time we spend on the phone," he suggested with an edge of sarcasm. "What the hell does time have to do with anything? Some people meet and get married practically overnight."

"That's very romantic. Then they discover all the problems."

"And they work them out."

"Or they get divorced. I'd rather resolve the big ones before I make any vows, thank you very much. One divorce in a lifetime is about all I can handle."

Dillon finally relented. If he'd learned nothing else about Catherine, it was that once she'd made up her mind, only gentle persuasion, not bulldozer tactics were effective. Maybe if he thought of this as an advertising campaign, he'd be more successful. He was the product. Catherine was the target audience. All he had to do was convince her that her life wouldn't be complete without one Dillon Ryan in the house. For a man with his collection of advertising awards, it should be a snap.

As it turned out, it wasn't. The campaign was sabotaged before it could even get into high gear. He made the mistake of calling his office from a pay phone at the deli. It was a compulsive habit. He did it without thinking of the consequences. Naturally there was a crisis. There was always a crisis.

"I'll get back to you in twenty minutes," he promised his secretary. "See if you can arrange a meeting for this afternoon."

By the time he returned to the table, his mind was already at work. He dragged out a leather-bound pocket notepad and began jotting down ideas.

"You called the office," Catherine accused.

Dillon regarded her guiltily. "Yes."

"You're on vacation."

"That doesn't mean I don't continue to have responsibilities."

"I thought you left Evan in charge."

"I did, but . . ."

"Dillon, how do you expect him to become a partner, if you don't let him handle the day-to-day work?"

"I am letting him handle it. I'm just giving him a little input," he said defensively.

She sat back in the booth. "What time's the meeting?"

"Who said anything about a meeting?"

"I know the way your mind works. Input equals meeting. What time?"

Dillon didn't want to give her the satisfaction of admitting she was right. Unfortunately there was no alternative. "I'm not sure," he said. "Helene is setting it up."

"And what about our New Year's Eve plans with the kids? They're going to be at your apartment at three o'clock expecting to spend the night with us. We promised them video games, movies and pizza."

"Damn, I forgot about that," he muttered. "It's okay, though. You'll be there and I won't be at the office more than an hour. Two tops. I may even get back before they arrive." He took her hand. "I'm sorry, sweetheart. I know this isn't fair to you. I'll keep the meeting short, so you won't be stuck with the boys alone for too long."

"Jonathan and Kevin are not the issue. We'll have a wonderful time together. I'm looking forward to seeing them. They, however, are counting on seeing you."

Guilt increased his defensiveness. Since the divorce, he'd made an honest effort not to disappoint the boys. "Catherine, it's not as though I'm cancelling anything. What's the big deal?"

She sighed and shook her head. "You honestly don't see it, do you?"

"And apparently you can't accept that this is the way I am. I will always live up to my obligations."

"Your business obligations," she corrected. "Family obligations seem to take a back seat."

Thoroughly frustrated by her refusal to understand, he slid out of the booth and threw some money on the table. "I'm going to the office. I'll be home when I can get there."

At the door of the deli, he turned back for just an instant. Catherine was sitting ramrod straight in the booth, angrily tearing napkins into shreds. As if she'd suddenly realized he was watching, she looked up and the expression in her eyes almost broke his heart. She looked like a woman who'd just lost everything important in her life.

Dillon knew exactly how she felt.

Catherine let herself into Dillon's apartment with the key he'd given her when they'd arrived from Atlanta. In the hour before the boys were due to arrive, she took a long, hot bath and questioned every angry word she'd uttered at Dillon. Was she being so unreasonable to expect him to balance work and his life with her and his sons? Was she a harridan for being concerned that his compulsive, type-A personality was a danger to his health?

Maybe the truth of the matter was that he was too much like Matthew and not nearly enough like her father. Rawley Devereaux had been born into family wealth. Though he worked every day of his life to maintain the family's financial position, he'd never had to scramble. Catherine had led a secure, moneyed life. Her father had made it seem easily attainable. Matthew hadn't had to claw his way to the top of the medical profession. He'd been naturally talented. He'd been to good schools. Everything had fallen into place for him, except the social position he'd wanted badly enough to marry her to get. Once he'd had money and a place in Atlanta society, he'd been free to indulge in the one thing he really loved: surgery. He'd spent all but the few hours he needed for sleep in the operating room.

Still debating about the best way to handle this afternoon's argument, she dressed in a hip-length red cashmere sweater and black wool slacks. She deliberately brushed her hair back in a smooth style that Dillon hated. He called it her country club look and said it made him nervous. Good, she thought, as she fastened it back with a black velvet clip. He ought to be nervous. He ought to be shaking in his boots. Guilty as sin. He ought to be...

Before she could think up any worse fates, the doorbell rang, followed by the noisy arrival of Jonathan and Kevin.

"Hey, Dad, we're here. You in the den?" Jonathan called.

Catherine met them in the hall.

"Hey, you two. Happy New Year!"

"Yeah," Kevin said, running to throw his arms around her. "We get to stay up 'til midnight? Are you gonna stay up, too?"

"I don't know," she teased, kneeling down to help him get off his boots. "That's pretty late for me. What about you, Jonathan? You think you'll be up that late?"

"Sure," he said, standing just a little straighter. "I'm nine now. I stay up late all the time."

"You're nine, huh? I thought you were eight just last month. That must mean you had a birthday."

"Yeah," he said. "I got some really neat stuff. You wanna see? I kept some of it here." He peered into the den. "Hey, where's Dad?"

"He had to stop by the office for a little while. He should be back shortly."

Kevin's eyes widened to big round circles. "Uh-oh, Mom's gonna be mad. We're not supposed to be here if Dad's not here."

"I'm sure it'll be okay, since I'm here," Catherine said, wondering if that were really true. The boys were being supervised by an adult, but Paula didn't know her. She very well might be furious. "Maybe I should call her. What do you think?"

"I'll call Dad," Jonathan said. "Maybe he can call her."

Catherine nodded. It was his responsibility, after all. "Okay, you call your father. Kevin, why don't you show me how to make some popcorn?"

"Don't you know?"

"I've done it before, but you're probably much better at it than I am."

"Okay," he said solemnly. "I'll help."

"You get started then wait for me to remove the bag from the oven," Catherine added. He ran off to the kitchen, while she lingered as Jonathan placed his call to Dillon's office.

"Hi, Aunt Helene. It's Jonathan. Is my dad there?"

His expression grew increasingly troubled. "Okay. Uh-huh. Okay. Bye."

"Everything okay?" Catherine asked.

"She said Dad's in a meeting."

Catherine felt her blood begin to race furiously. "You didn't talk to your father at all?"

"She asked me if I was here and said she'd have him call me the minute he got out of the meeting."

"Damn!" she muttered without thinking. She felt a small hand patting her arm.

"It's okay, Catherine. Mom won't mind that you're baby-sitting us."

"What if it had been an emergency?" she said, helpless in the face of his nine-year-old aplomb.

"I would have told her, that's all. Dad told me to be sure and tell her if it was really, really important and he would always take the call. I figured this wasn't an emergency. We're just fine here with you."

She reached out and hugged him. "Yes, Jonathan. You are just fine with me. Now let's see how Kevin's coming with the popcorn."

When Dillon still wasn't back by seven, Catherine called out for the pizza. They'd finished it and played three different video games by the time he finally walked through the door. She had to steel herself not to react to the exhaustion she could see in his eyes. She had to be equally adept to hide her fury.

Jonathan and Kevin greeted him exuberantly, apparently unbothered by his failure to get home sooner. He scooped Kevin into his arms and ruffled Jonathan's dark curls.

"We've been having a great time, Dad," Jonathan said. "Catherine's real good at video games."

He stared at her over Kevin's head. "I'll bet she is. Did you guys leave me any pizza?"

"It's in the oven," she said. "I'll get it."

"Thanks, babe."

When she returned to the den, he was on the floor helping Kevin compete with Jonathan in yet another video game. Though the tired lines around his eyes were more pronounced than ever, he had one arm around Kevin. His attention was completely focused on the game. It was yet another indication that Dillon was a compulsive competitor, no matter the forum. Even a children's game required his total energy. He lifted his head and turned the full force of his smile on her as he accepted the pizza.

"Wine?" she asked.

"I think I'd better have something with caffeine in it, if I'm going to stay awake 'til midnight."

"Coffee or a soda?"

"A soda."

When she returned with the soft drink, she tried to stay aloof, but it was no time before Jonathan had drawn her into the game on his side, declaring that Kevin had an unfair advantage. "You've got to help, Catherine. Dad's vicious."

"So I see," she murmured. "Let's see what we can do about that."

A half hour later, when she and Jonathan emerged victorious, Dillon laughed. "Tamed at last," he said.

"Hardly tamed, I'm afraid."

"Boys, why don't you go get those horns and things I bought for New Year's? They're in your room." When they were gone, he leaned over and kissed her. "I'm sorry about earlier."

Catherine sighed and ran her fingertips over the lines on his face. "You look exhausted."

"I am."

"Dillon, why..."

"We'll talk about it later," he promised. "I'll try to explain. I owe you that much at least."

"Then you are aware of what you're doing to yourself?"

He nodded, then managed a bright smile as his sons returned and engaged him in more rambunctious horseplay. If it weren't for the serious talk hanging over them, Catherine would have been thoroughly content. This was the family she'd always wanted. The boys had welcomed her into their lives as naturally and easily as any woman could ever hope. If she accepted Dillon's oft-repeated proposal, she would be with the man she loved, with his children, maybe even with a child of their own. That was so much; more than many women ever had. Why was she clinging so stubbornly to the one flaw in the arrangement?

Because it wasn't some tiny, incidental character trait. It wasn't that Dillon left his socks on the floor or his whiskers in the sink. Socks were easily picked up. Whiskers could be washed away. A husband who was never around, who put his job above his marriage was something else entirely.

"Catherine, look," Kevin said excitedly. "It's almost midnight. That big ball is starting to move."

The television announcers and the mob in Times Square rang in the new year. Kevin and Jonathan blew their horns. Dillon drew her into his arms. "Happy New Year, sweetheart!"

"Happy New Year," she said, tears streaming down her cheeks. If only they could capture this moment, maybe it would indeed be a happy new year.

When the boys were in bed at last, Dillon pulled her down on the sofa beside him.

"Dillon, maybe this should wait until tomorrow. It's nearly 1:00 a.m."

"No. You'd better catch me while I'm feeling mellow. This isn't something I normally talk about."

Catherine's heart filled with dread. He looked so sad. "What, Dillon? Don't you know there's nothing you can't tell me?"

"I know that. I know you want to understand what makes me the way I am about business. It all started thirty years ago."

"But you were just a boy then."

"That's right. Just about Jonathan's age. Very impressionable. My father lost his job. It happens to a lot of men, right? The company was badly managed. It went into bankruptcy and my father was out on the streets. At first he and Mom tried to hide that there was anything wrong. He left the house every day looking for a new job. But he was older. His skills were becoming obsolete. He was willing to take job skills training, but there weren't so many programs for that then. He took odd jobs. My mother took in laundry and cleaned houses. We survived, but my father was never okay after that. We never stopped loving him, but he lost respect for himself. A man can't survive that."

It wasn't so much Dillon's words that moved Catherine as the haunted expression in his eyes, the sadness of his memories. "It must have been terrible for all of you."

"Just a lesson. I swore I would never be dependent on another human being for an income, that whatever business I was in, I would own it."

"You've done that, darling. You're successful. Your business is flourishing."

"I have to see that it stays there, not just for myself, Catherine. Not even for the boys. I have employees. Over a hundred of them now, here and in Los Angeles. I have a responsibility to them, too, and to their families."

It was too much, Catherine thought, far too much burden for one man to shoulder alone. But she understood at last; she could feel his need to stay on top, to provide for those who'd been loyal to him.

"Dillon, couldn't you share some of that responsibility?"

"It's mine, Catherine. I accepted that the day I opened the doors of the business."

"And what if you ruin your health? What if you drive yourself so hard that you have a heart attack and die?" she said angrily. "Who will be responsible for all those people then, Dillon? Who will see that they're provided for? Are you so sure that you're not being selfish? You're everyone's hero. You're sacrificing your life to see that all those people have food on their tables. It must make you feel wonderful. If you had to share that, it would lessen your role as hero, wouldn't it? But I ask you again, what if you kill yourself in the process? Who'll be the hero then? And what in God's name will your sons and I do without you?''

# Ten

---

*Valentine's Day*

"**H**ave you heard from Dillon today?" Beth Markham asked as Catherine paced up and down the jammed aisles of St. Christopher's tiny thrift shop idly picking up merchandise and putting it back again. "Cat, some of that stuff is practically threadbare as it is. If you keep fiddling with it, it will fall apart. Why don't you just sit down and tell me what's on your mind?"

"I can't sit down," she said. She continued pacing, but she kept her hands to herself. Beth waited patiently, until finally Catherine admitted, "I think I've made a terrible mistake."

"What mistake?"

"I told Dillon he was killing himself and that I'd never marry him unless he stopped it."

"Okay," Beth said slowly, as she obviously struggled to absorb the implications of the blunt pronouncement. "I think I get it. What's so terrible about that?"

"What if he can't? It's a long story, but all his life Dillon's had this terrible need in him to succeed. What if he can't ever put it into perspective?"

"Have you talked to him about this?"

"I haven't talked to him at all, not since I left New York after New Year's. He hasn't called once."

"I see. Tell me something, Cat. If you had it to do all over again, would you still fall in love with Dillon?"

Catherine grinned. "I wasn't aware that we got to choose the people we fall in love with."

"Now you sound like me," Beth chastised. "You know what I mean. When you first met Dillon, you didn't even know his last name. He didn't know how to find you. You could have left it like that. It would have been some lovely romantic memory. Knowing what you know now, would you have done anything differently? Would you have ended it right then?"

She thought about that, remembered how much stronger and more self-confident she was for knowing Dillon, how much love she'd felt in his arms. "No."

"Why? What was it about the man you met that night that drew you?"

"He was warm and supportive and attentive. He made me feel incredibly special in a way I had never felt before."

"Do you still have times like that?"

"Some," she said, beginning to understand the point Beth was trying to make. "Mostly in Savannah."

"Then it seems to me that the answer is obvious."

"I don't think I can talk Dillon into moving to Savannah. Not in a million years. The one time I even broached the possibility of his leaving New York, he threw a fit."

"What if he opened up a branch office down there? He already has a couple of accounts in Savannah, doesn't he? It would be a natural step. I don't know all that much about advertising, but wouldn't it give him a presence in the southeast?"

"It makes sense to me, but he really seems adamant about staying in New York. I'm not sure he'd even listen to the idea."

"Maybe he would if you present it properly, say with a little wine and candlelight. It seems to me like Valentine's Day would be a good time to try."

"What would I do without you?" Catherine said as the idea took hold and began to blossom. She hugged Beth in an unusual display of affection. "Thank you. You're wonderful."

"Just trying to keep my rating as the best matchmaker in town."

"You didn't introduce me to Dillon," she reminded her. "You don't even know him."

"But who sent you back to Savannah to see him again? Who pushed you to move down there so you could see him more often?"

"Okay, okay," she said, laughing. "If it works out, you get the credit."

"I don't want credit, just an invitation to the wedding."

"You've got it. Keep your fingers crossed for me, will you?"

"I always do. Something tells me that this time you don't need it."

"I hope you're right. I really do."

Catherine packed her bag without the slightest regard for neatness. She tossed it into the back of the car, then ran back inside to call Dillon's office.

"Mrs. Devlin," Helene said, clearly surprised to be hearing from her. "How are you?"

"I'm just fine, Helene. Is Mr. Ryan in?"

"No. I'm terribly sorry, but you just missed him. He left on a business trip."

Catherine had to bite back her disappointment. Maybe it was better this way. Maybe it would be more effective if she didn't speak to Dillon directly. If he was furious with her, a message passed through a third party might be more likely to get his attention.

"Can you reach him?"

"Of course."

"Then please tell him that I must see him at once. It's urgent. I'm leaving Atlanta now and I should be back in Savannah by midafternoon. Can you get that message to him?"

"Right away, but . . ."

Catherine hung up before the secretary could say anything that might dissuade her from her plan. The last thing she needed to hear was that Dillon's trip was also urgent or that he'd flown off to Los Angeles to engage in mortal combat to save Ruben Prunelli's soul.

The tedious drive to Savannah had never taken longer. All during the five-and-a-half-hour trip she went over her arguments, trying to brace herself for the moment when she'd have to use them to convince Dillon that this could work, that they could have a life together without sacrificing his needs or hers.

By the time she'd parked in front of the carriage house, she was sure she could make it work. Two hours later, when Dillon still hadn't called, her faith began to waver. She began to cook. She chopped. She minced. She stirred. Like therapy, she found it soothing. She'd made coq au vin, a salad that could have served all the tourists in town, fresh rolls and three pies. She was considering baking a cake, when she heard the scrape of a key in the lock. She froze. Despite all her pep talks, she wasn't ready to face him.

"Catherine?"

"In the kitchen," she said breathlessly.

When she finally found nerve enough to turn around, he was standing in the doorway. His dark hair was windblown, his tie was askew. He looked very much like a man who'd rushed to get there. He looked wonderful.

"You look wonderful," he said quietly.

"Thank you."

"I've missed you."

"I've missed you too."

"I've been thinking," they said together, then laughed nervously.

"You first," she said.

"Maybe we should have some wine. Do you have a bottle?"

"In the dining room." While he was gone, she clung to the counter and dragged in a deep breath. She was determined to be composed when she faced him again. She was determined he would never see how just the sight of him had shaken her.

"Catherine," he said softly.

She whirled around and found herself nearly in his arms. Their gazes collided and held. She swallowed hard and tried not to back away.

"Your wine." He held out the glass. She took it, careful not to allow their fingers to brush. The temperature in the kitchen had already risen several degrees. One touch was all it would take to set her blood on fire. One touch would ignite all of the old passions and they would never say the words that had to be spoken.

"To warm thoughts," he said, his eyes never leaving hers.

She pulled her gaze away and sipped desperately at the wine. It only made her hotter, more uncertain. She'd longed to seem cool. She'd wanted desperately to be bold. Instead, she was simply Catherine. For better or worse.

"I've been thinking," he said again. "I've made some decisions."

"Oh."

"The past six weeks have been the most miserable I've ever spent in my life. I finally had to do some serious reevaluating of my goals."

"And? What did you come up with?"

He leaned nonchalantly against the counter. His carefully chosen words belied the casual stance. "It all kept coming back to you. I don't want to lose you."

She bit her lip to keep from crying out. She clung to the wineglass to keep from throwing her arms around him. She waited, tension spreading through her, hope held desperately at bay.

"I've finally sat down and had a long talk with Evan about the company. As a result, he's now a full partner. He's going to run the New York office. He can't handle it all alone yet, but it's a start."

"He must be very happy," she said cautiously.

"I've also decided to open an office here in Savannah. I have two clients here now and prospects seem good for more. I'll still have to travel to New York and Los Angeles, but I should be able to change my pace quite a bit if everything works out with Evan."

Catherine felt a wave of relief wash through her, followed by one nagging suspicion. The timing of this seemed very odd. Was it possible that Beth had called Dillon and prodded him into making these radical changes today, the same notions that had been planted in her mind by a worried friend?

She cleared her throat. "Um, when did you decide all this?"

"Evan and I started talking about it about two weeks after you left. The pieces finally fell into place today. I took the first plane out to tell you about it."

Catherine had to fight off the desire to laugh hysterically. Today! He'd finalized the plans today. But he'd made the decision on his own, reached the same exact conclusion she had reached.

"Well," he said. "You're not saying anything. What do you think?"

"I think . . ." She began to grin. She could feel the smile growing wider and wider. "I think this is the most wonderful news I've ever had in my life," she said, no longer fighting her elation.

"Are you sure?" he said, regarding her hesitantly.

"Oh, Dillon, I've never been more certain of anything in my life. We'll be happy here. I know we will. We can go to New York as often as you want to see your sons. We can find a house. The boys can have their own rooms for when they come to visit. I'll sell the one in Atlanta. It's going to be perfect."

He seemed to be struggling with an emotion every bit as powerful as what she was feeling. "I was so afraid," he admitted in a choked voice. He pulled her into his arms and held her. "If I'd lost you, Catherine, I don't know what I would have done."

"But you didn't lose me. There wasn't a single minute that I didn't believe that we would find a way to work it out."

He leaned back and regarded her so skeptically that she finally smiled. "Okay, maybe there were one or two minutes, when I had a few doubts. It didn't last."

"I don't know why it took me so long to see it," he said. "I've liked Savannah more and more each time I've been here. The work I've been doing for White Stone is some of the best I've ever done. Most important, you're happy here. Evan suggested I locate the office in Atlanta, but I like the idea that this will be a fresh start for both of us in the city where we met."

"I agree."

"You won't mind not being in Atlanta?"

"No. My ties there have loosened with every week I've been away. My parents won't be happy, but it's not as if I'll be at the ends of the earth. They'll adjust."

"Your father may, but your mother? I'm not so sure."

"She'll grumble, but if we offer her two new grandsons to spoil, it should make up for my absence."

"Two? You are ambitious."

"I meant Jonathan and Kevin."

"What about their baby sister then?"

"I didn't know you were even pregnant," she teased him.

"Okay, enough. You're happy about Savannah. You'd enjoy working here after you finish school?"

"Absolutely, and best of all there are no ghosts here. Just long, lazy days to build a new life together."

"Lazy?" he said, one brow lifting quizzically.

"Okay, bad choice of words. I won't ask for the impossible."

He touched her lips. "No, sweetheart. Always ask. Together, even the impossible seems within reach."

# Epilogue

## May 16

"**I** simply don't understand why you insisted on getting married on May 16," Lucinda Devereaux told Catherine as she rearranged her veil. "It's the middle of the week. No one can take off to come clear down here for a wedding."

"We met on May 16 two years ago," Catherine explained patiently as she put the veil back the way it had been. "And I don't know how you can complain about the guest list. You must have had two hundred acceptances. The owner of the restaurant is ecstatic."

"I should think he would be," her mother said haughtily. "It's probably more business than he usually gets in an entire week."

"Hardly. It's a very popular restaurant."

"It's a seafood place, Catherine. No one holds a wedding reception in a seafood restaurant."

"Maybe no Devereaux does, but the Ryans of New York, Atlanta and Savannah do. It has a sentimental meaning for us."

"I suppose that's where you met."

"It is."

"I just hope they aired it out. I'd hate to have all our guests smelling like catfish."

"Mother, stop fussing. Go talk to Dad or something. I want to find Dillon."

"Dillon? For heaven sakes, Catherine, you can't see him before the wedding."

"Oh, but I can," she said, marching off.

"Catherine!"

She turned back. "Think of it this way, Mother. I'm setting new trends."

"You're playing havoc with traditions."

She found Dillon trying to tie Kevin's bow tie. He was making a real mess of it. "Let me," she said, pushing him aside. "You look very handsome, Kevin. You, too, Jonathan."

"What about me?" Dillon demanded.

"I'm not supposed to look at you."

"You've obviously been talking to your mother again. She is not happy that there's no full orchestra to play the wedding march."

"She'll have to learn to live with the flute and the trumpet."

"How did you ever find those two musicians we heard on our first real date?"

"A desperate woman can accomplish miracles."

"The ad in the paper helped," Beth noted, coming up behind them. "I don't suppose you all would like to get this show on the road?"

"What's the matter?" Catherine teased. "Don't you get full credit for your matchmaking talent until after the ceremony?"

"Matchmaking?" Dillon repeated, his expression confused. "Do I know this woman?"

"No, but you will," Beth promised. "I will remind you until the day you die how much you owe me. Without me, Catherine might never have had the nerve to try and convince you to move to Savannah."

"Beth!" Catherine protested weakly.

The warning came too late. Dillon had already picked up on the remark. Beth looked from one to the other and moaned. "Uh-oh."

"Indeed," Catherine said.

"I think I'd better go check the flowers."

"Good idea."

"What was she talking about?" Dillon demanded.

"You remember Valentine's Day?"

"The day I came down here after you."

"Well, I never did mention that I'd called your office that morning and I guess Helene never mentioned it, either, because you never said anything, right?"

"I'm with you so far."

"Remember I told you that I'd been thinking, but then I told you to go first?"

"I think I remember something like that."

"Well, I had decided that I was going to try and convince you to move to Savannah and open an office. Beth prodded me into at least talking the idea over with you. I told Helene I needed to see you urgently. When you came in, I thought that was why you were here."

Dillon started chuckling when she was halfway through telling him. "I guess my announcement must really have thrown you for a loop."

"You could say that."

"It just proves one thing."

"What's that?"

"Two minds that much in tune belong together. We'll be unbeatable."

"You bet we will," she said softly just as his mouth closed over hers. The kiss was filled with all the tenderness, all the love that Dillon had to offer.

It was definitely the beginning of forever.

\*     \*     \*     \*     \*

The tradition continues this month as Silhouette presents its fifth annual Christmas collection

SILHOUETTE

Christmas

STORIES 1990

The romance of Christmas sparkles in four enchanting stories written by some of your favorite Silhouette authors:

Ann Major * SANTA'S SPECIAL MIRACLE
Rita Rainville * LIGHTS OUT!
Lindsay McKenna * ALWAYS AND FOREVER
Kathleen Creighton * THE MYSTERIOUS GIFT

Spend the holidays with Silhouette and discover the special magic of falling in love in this heartwarming Christmas collection.

## ARE YOU A ROMANCE READER WITH OPINIONS?

Openings are currently available for participation in the 1990-1991 Romance Reader Panel. We are looking for new participants from all regions of the country and from all age ranges.

If selected, you will be polled once a month by mail to comment on new books you have recently purchased, and may occasionally be asked for more in-depth comments. Individual responses will remain confidential and all postage will be prepaid.

Regular purchasers of one favorite series, as well as those who sample a variety of lines each month, are needed, so fill out and return this application today for more detailed information.

1. Please indicate the romance series you purchase from regularly at retail outlets.

| Harlequin | Silhouette | |
|---|---|---|
| 1. ☐ Romance | 6. ☐ Romance | 10. ☐ Bantam Loveswept |
| 2. ☐ Presents | 7. ☐ Special Edition | 11. ☐ Other _____ |
| 3. ☐ American Romance | 8. ☐ Intimate Moments | |
| 4. ☐ Temptation | 9. ☐ Desire | |
| 5. ☐ Superromance | | |

2. Number of romance paperbacks you purchase new in an average month:

   12.1 ☐ 1 to 4        .2 ☐ 5 to 10        .3 ☐ 11 to 15        .4 ☐ 16+

3. Do you currently buy romance                    13.1 ☐ yes        .2 ☐ no
   series through direct mail?

   If yes, please indicate series: _____
                                                              (14,15)      (16,17)

4. Date of birth: _____ / _____ / _____
                  (Month)    (Day)    (Year)
                   18,19     20,21     22,23

5. Please print:
   Name: _____
   Address: _____
   City: _____ State: _____ Zip: _____
   Telephone No. (optional): ( _____ )

MAIL TO: Attention: Romance Reader Panel
         Consumer Opinion Center
         P.O. Box 1395
         Buffalo, NY 14240-9961            ☐☐☐☐☐☐☐☐☐☐☐☐☐

                                           **Office Use Only**      DDK

# Take 4 bestselling love stories FREE

## Plus get a FREE surprise gift!

# PASSPORT TO ROMANCE
# SWEEPSTAKES RULES

1. **HOW TO ENTER:** To enter, you must be the age of majority and complete the official entry form, or print your name, address, telephone number and age on a plain piece of paper and mail to: Passport to Romance, P.O. Box 9056, Buffalo, NY 14269-9056. No mechanically reproduced entries accepted.

2. All entries must be received by the CONTEST CLOSING DATE, DECEMBER 31, 1990 TO BE ELIGIBLE.

3. **THE PRIZES:** There will be ten (10) Grand Prizes awarded, each consisting of a choice of a trip for two people from the following list:
   i) London, England (approximate retail value $5,050 U.S.)
   ii) England, Wales and Scotland (approximate retail value $6,400 U.S.)
   iii) Carribean Cruise (approximate retail value $7,300 U.S.)
   iv) Hawaii (approximate retail value $9,550 U.S.)
   v) Greek Island Cruise in the Mediterranean (approximate retail value $12,250 U.S.)
   vi) France (approximate retail value $7,300 U.S.)

4. Any winner may choose to receive any trip or a cash alternative prize of $5,000.00 U.S. in lieu of the trip.

5. **GENERAL RULES:** Odds of winning depend on number of entries received.

6. A random draw will be made by Nielsen Promotion Services, an independent judging organization, on January 29, 1991, in Buffalo, NY, at 11:30 a.m. from all eligible entries received on or before the Contest Closing Date.

7. Any Canadian entrants who are selected must correctly answer a time-limited, mathematical skill-testing question in order to win.

8. Full contest rules may be obtained by sending a stamped, self-addressed envelope to: "Passport to Romance Rules Request", P.O. Box 9998, Saint John, New Brunswick, Canada E2L 4N4.

9. Quebec residents may submit any litigation respecting the conduct and awarding of a prize in this contest to the Régie des loteries et courses du Québec.

10. Payment of taxes other than air and hotel taxes is the sole responsibility of the winner.

11. Void where prohibited by law.

# COUPON BOOKLET OFFER TERMS

To receive your Free travel-savings coupon booklets, complete the mail-in Offer Certificate on the preceeding page, including the necessary number of proofs-of-purchase, and mail to: Passport to Romance, P.O. Box 9057, Buffalo, NY 14269-9057. The coupon booklets include savings on travel-related products such as car rentals, hotels, cruises, flowers and restaurants. Some restrictions apply. The offer is available in the United States and Canada. Requests must be postmarked by January 25, 1991. Only proofs-of-purchase from specially marked "Passport to Romance" Harlequin® or Silhouette® books will be accepted. The offer certificate must accompany your request and may not be reproduced in any manner. Offer void where prohibited or restricted by law. LIMIT FOUR COUPON BOOKLETS PER NAME, FAMILY, GROUP, ORGANIZATION OR ADDRESS. Please allow up to 8 weeks after receipt of order for shipment. Enter quickly as quantities are limited. Unfulfilled mail-in offer requests will receive free Harlequin® or Silhouette® books (not previously available in retail stores), in quantities equal to the number of proofs-of-purchase required for Levels One to Four, as applicable.

PR-SWPS

## OFFICIAL SWEEPSTAKES ENTRY FORM

Complete and return this Entry Form immediately—the more Entry Forms you submit, the better your chances of winning!
- Entry Forms must be received by **December 31, 1990**
- A random draw will take place on **January 29, 1991**        3-SD-3-SW
- Trip must be taken by **December 31, 1991**

YES, I want to win a PASSPORT TO ROMANCE vacation for two! I understand the prize includes round-trip air fare, accommodation and a daily spending allowance.

Name_____

Address_____

City_____ State_____ Zip_____

Telephone Number_____ Age_____

Return entries to: **PASSPORT TO ROMANCE**, P.O. Box 9056, Buffalo, NY 14269-9056

© 1990 Harlequin Enterprises Limited

## COUPON BOOKLET/OFFER CERTIFICATE

| Item | LEVEL ONE Booklet 1 | LEVEL TWO Booklet 1 & 2 | LEVEL THREE Booklet 1, 2 & 3 | LEVEL FOUR Booklet 1, 2, 3 & 4 |
|---|---|---|---|---|
| Booklet 1 = $100+ | $100+ | $100+ | $100+ | $100+ |
| Booklet 2 = $200+ | | $200+ | $200+ | $200+ |
| Booklet 3 = $300+ | | | $300+ | $300+ |
| Booklet 4 = $400+ | ____ | ____ | ____ | $400+ |
| Approximate Total Value of Savings | $100+ | $300+ | $600+ | $1,000+ |
| # of Proofs of Purchase Required | 4 | 6 | 12 | 18 |
| Check One | ____ | ____ | ____ | ____ |

Name_____

Address_____

City_____ State_____ Zip_____

Return Offer Certificates to: **PASSPORT TO ROMANCE**, P.O. Box 9057, Buffalo, NY 14269-9057

Requests must be postmarked by **January 25, 1991**

- - - - - - - - - - - - - - - - - - - - - - - - - - - - - - ✂ - - - -

## ONE PROOF OF PURCHASE        3-SD-3

To collect your free coupon booklet you must include the necessary number of proofs-of-purchase with a properly completed Offer Certificate
© 1990 Harlequin Enterprises Limited

See previous page for details